To Anthony. Thank you for believing in me.

"Our life is made by the death of others."

— Leonardo da Vinci

Prologue

The Banumi were a race of demon peacekeepers. Protectors by nature, it was their duty to defend the defenseless. Humans were the weakest race, and the demons became their permanent guard. Two powerful tribes, the Allu and Phytian, had been warring for time immemorial. The Allu were thought of as receiving their gifts from water, the Phytian from fire. In truth, both tribes shared a very rare anomaly within their DNA, an extra chromosome that defined the tribes' powers. The powers expressed themselves through bijous that were passed down from parent to child. Humans were completely ignorant either tribe existed and their infiltration of human ranks was common. The Banumi power was completely internal.

It was said the Allu and Phytians lived as one. Sorin Broniche scoffed at such an idea. He was the oldest being on the planet and the last of the Banumi. He'd never seen such. Blood and death had always been a constant between the two tribes. His race ended many battles between the Allu and Phytians during times of war. One powerful demon could stop a battle of hundreds.

No one expected the tribes to come together for the sole purpose of exterminating their mutual interloper. But by working together the tribes outnumbered the Banumi. There were many massacres, many clans slaughtered.

Only a few elite managed to hide. Even fewer could protect their human charges. Insult to injury, humans evolved and began to think of their peaceful defenders as enemies, calling them dragons and destroying the last of their protectors.

After losing his best friend, Mikhail, Sorin decided there was nothing he could do except go into estivation, a self-induced trance that focused the mind. While one was in trance, the earth provided for every need and rejuvenated the body. Most who practiced remained in the state for an extended period. It was not an easy thing to endure or so Sorin heard. His father warned him one could see others in need of defending but were unable to aid. You were there in spirit and had to watch the atrocities of the world take place before your eyes. You saw plagues of the past, wars of the future and murders of the youth with no way to track where the immoral acts were occurring. Fully waking out of a trance could take hours if not days. In short, it was a punishment. It was failing.

Sorin was no stranger to failure and disappointment. The Phytian beat the Allu into submission. His race was now thought as mythical. He was mentally and physically tired.

It came as a shock when he found himself impervious to the reaper's scythe. There were legends of the elders becoming immortal but he had not thought them true. But over the past century, Sorin tried countless times to take his own life and failed.

He was sure having a moiety would give him some semblance of mortality again but he knew also that his death would end her life as well. Moieties were intended to make their mates stronger. He wanted to die and the death of one's mate was the death of one's self. He hoped he didn't have one.

"There is nothing like having a mate. It is as if you are tall as a mountain and small as an insect," Mikhail said to him long ago.

"*Who wants to be an insect?*" Sorin thought. The loss of his friend was the bitterest of pills to swallow. Mikhail found his moiety early in life. He'd made a point to marry her in the human way as well. They had four children and were happy until he was exposed as a Banumi. The Phytian savagely murdered Mikhail along with his children. His mate died the instant his heart stopped.

Anyone not born in Sorin's century would be a hindrance, he thought. There was no way his soulmate was alive all this time and not come to him. Besides, with the tribes killing each other, mates being found without bijou and the birth of children to moieties was almost nonexistent. Only true mates — moieties — could procreate.

Sorin shook his head. Every race was shot to hell if something did not change. He morphed into his demon form and rested on a large boulder by a thin stream of lava. The extreme heat soothed him. He took in one last breath, closed his eyes and started to chant.

6

1990

AMARYL

Amaryl Kier had been coming to the mountain for months. It was hidden among seven taller ones—making it the perfect place to hone her abilities.

Many wondered where she retreated after receiving the news of her upcoming marriage to Murdox Zorn. None had the nerve to follow her—Murdox was the head of the Phytian tribe and a complete brute. They were betrothed, but he was not her mate. Her family was optimistic everything would turn out for the best, but she was doubtful. Besides being disgusted by his attitude and disposition, his leadership skills were atrocious. He was a dictator. Ruling with an iron fist, wrist, forearm. His entire right arm was covered by the world's largest bijou, which multiplied his power.

Amaryl loathed him. Who needs that much power? She was not mad at her parents for giving their blessing. They had no other choice. Either they would hand over their oldest daughter or die.

She sighed. She would do what was best for the family but she didn't have to like it. At least she could save other girls from such a sad fate, including her twin sister, Anabel.

After three weeks, Amaryl showed great progress at levitating large stones with her mind and guiding them into a large crater. Over the past week, she'd added a new element—setting the projectiles ablaze. Looking around, she noticed her supply was dwindling. She would have to go into the mouth of the crater and bring some topside. That would require another skill—levitating herself.

Floating your own body was a rare talent and no one knew she could do it. She was still a novice, but she was willing to try. Of course, if she failed, she could die.

After ten minutes of hanging in midair, Amaryl found the floor of the crater by crash-landing on her butt. Her new acid-washed jeans were ruined but she was alive. When she looked around, it wasn't just a crater like she'd thought—more a mysterious cavern.

Barely making out shapes, she threw flame at the boulder and lit it, and then hurled it toward the opening above. Surprise gripped her at the amount of mental strength it took to get the one large rock to the top. Gravity was working against her. She had not been this tired in weeks and it made her angry. Stomping her foot, Amaryl lit the entire collection of granite in a fit of temper. When she turned her back to the blaze, her breath caught. In the farthest corner of the cavern sat a massive onyx Banumi statue.

Why would anyone put such a beautiful sculpture here? She spent a few minutes pondering that while studying it from every angle. The details were amazing. It took only moments before the urge to touch it became overwhelming.

The feel of its smooth texture gave way to an even brighter notion of climbing the sleeping beast. She laughed. It was her personal pony. Well, maybe not, but it was a great place to rest while regaining her strength.

The Phytians had legends about amazing creatures, demons called Banumi. They were said to have gone extinct during the main stint of the war. Humans named them dragons out of ignorance and the derogatory title stuck.

She laughed again. The only thing differentiating humans from the tribes now were bloodlines and weapons. Humans were not only ignorant of the existence of bijous but also their power. Even among the Phytians and Allu, bijous were as rare as blue unicorns.

Rumor had it Zorn was killing his own people to steal the strength from their bijou to add to his monstrosity. If that were true, not only was it against the sacred laws of both tribes, but it would make Zorn the strongest being in the world. It was just a fable like the boogieman. Something to tell your misbehaving children.

"The jerk would have to be my future husband," Amaryl grumbled to her new companion. She lay there talking aloud to it for the next two hours. All her fears and her dreams hung heavy in the air but she felt better once they were out. "You were a great listener, Godzilla," she confessed while dismounting.

Bending to kiss its snout in thanks, she watched as the stone blinked and focused on her. She froze. She found herself staring into amazing golden eyes. Seconds turned to a full minute before her screams rattled the walls and the floor rose up to smack her in the face.

GABRIELA

A hard slap ripped me from a night terror. "Dammit, Madison," I gasped. "Do that shit again and I will force-feed you Hector's cooking for a week."

"Well, I had to do something. You were screaming so loud I thought the neighbors would think I was pulling a Poe on you."

"A what?"

"You know, cutting you up and burying you under the floorboards," she explained. I blinked. She shrugged and left the room.

Madison "Maddie" Hart was my best friend and arch nemesis. We'd been close since the day she'd saved me from being attacked by a killer jacket. It was my first year of kindergarten when I'd caught a string around a tooth by chewing a hole in the sleeve of my windbreaker. The jacket and I had been fighting for twenty minutes in a corner.

"Are you okay?" a maze-haired girl asked. I shook my head.

"Can you talk?" she asked. I nodded.

"Well move your hand so we can be friends."

"I'm trying." I mumbled around my fist.

"You can't?" she asked. I shook my head again.

She gripped my arm with both her hands and pulled. With a pop, my arm was free. We smiled at each other. Seconds later her eyes widened and her friendly smile faded. Frowning, I lifted my hand to my lips. My tooth wasn't there. Looking at my sleeve, I saw not only had my arm been yanked away but so had my tooth. I poked the spot. My finger came away wet with blood.

"You get to meet the tooth fairy," the girl said and we giggled. We'd been inseparable ever since.

Maddie was used to the midnight audition for Scream Queens. The same nightmare haunted me each time. The same spewing and night sweats. The same tossing and turning. There were many nights I would not sleep, dreaming of drowning.

Because of it, when I was younger, I wouldn't go anywhere near water. Swimming pools and even bath tubs were totally out of the question. When I was fifteen, my psychologist suggested I take a few swimming lessons to overcome my aquaphobia. After attending only two classes, I was called a natural and my mom made me join the swim team.

Swimming in the ocean is still a huge no. The terrors never stopped but they did slow. Now at twenty-two, weekly screechings are the best I can hope for.

Maddie and I recently moved to my house in the Ocean Peak area of St. Simons Island. Mine was the family vacation home every year until my dad passed. Although I generally stayed away from the water, we'd bond over a warm fire pit and listen to the waves. The landscape with its tall grasses and sandy beaches changed with the tides. No one lived in the house for years and my mom refused to sell or rent it out. It used to be my dad's bachelor pad before he and Mom got married.

My dad, Lewis Blair, was one of the top pharmaceutical marketing managers in America and the best father in the history of all fathers. When he passed, his assets were split between my brother Trent and I. He got a swanky New York flat and the Los Angeles beach house. I got this place and a split-level in Phoenix. We both received a handsome trust.

Of everything, this three-bedroom house, with its butter-colored walls and large bay windows, was my favorite place in the world. The lawns were well manicured and fresh morning glory vines crept up to its roof. The scent of sea water blown in by the breeze was like a huge reset button, restarting the past few months. The stares, the growth spurt, the betrayals of the past were all gone.

Clambering out of bed, I headed to the kitchen, wrapping up in a silk robe. After eating a muffin and grabbing two quart-size Smartwaters, I headed to the basement for my morning workout. Madison had beaten me there. Slipping on my running gear, I pressed play on the speaker dock. Jacoby Shaddix began yelling about losing his sight and mind. It was a representation of what I'd been doing over the past few months.

The week before our move, I decided to go to the mall to pick up a few last minute items. I was thinking about the trip when a chance encounter with a stranger's arm changed everything. I slowed and gave the guy an apologetic smile.

A familiar voice echoing off the walls of the ladies' restroom caught my attention. I would have known that nasally tone anywhere. Katelyn.

I leaned against the door, listening. "I can't wait to see this house Gabriela keeps yapping about," the voice said.

I smiled. I had been a bit proud of it.

The voice continued. "All her bragging is making me hate her more. She thinks she is so great. I know it is going to be a titanic size bore but I don't have anything else to do this summer."

Another voice giggled. Gwyneth. "Moody much?"

"Don't act like you like her. You are just going to see if it is all she bragged about."

"I've never said I didn't like her," said Gwyneth.

"Your sister told me you don't want to go but because I was going, you felt trapped."

"No, I don't want to go but only because Gabriela told me she didn't want any guys at her new place. No guys equals no fun! Plus, I don't think she likes men and I am so not into girls. Who refuses Landon Grant? Did you see how he was staring at Amy's party last night? It was like she was famous or something. He's asked her out four times!"

"Yes, she isn't even pretty! It isn't just Landon either? Have you noticed when any guy asks her out she always says no? Like she has something better to do."

"She does—reading books. How funny! Four months ago she was totally invisible. I still think it's the car."

"No, I *told* you it was the plastic surgery," said Katelyn. It was clear they'd had this conversation before.

During the past six months, there had been a considerable number of changes to my body but surgery had not been one. In three months' time, I had grown at least four inches in height. Curves suddenly begun to appear on my boyish frame, giving me a completely foreign figure. Overnight, I'd jumped two full cup sizes. Even my hair changed—from a frizzy warm auburn with streaks of rust orange—to a wavy black that sometimes looked frightening against my pale green eyes and light skin. I tried to hide my new body most of the time by wearing one of the oversized traveler hoodies Trent sent to me. My mom tried to make me feel better by saying it was a growth spurt. I knew people had them when they were younger but not at my age.

The only perk to the insanity? I got a whole new wardrobe. I'd always considered myself as a cobweb—if you weren't looking for me, you would never know I was there—so being gawked at was new to me.

Until now, I thought the only change people noticed was my hair color. Katelyn and Gwyneth never mentioned the changes. Maybe if they'd happened to anyone else, I would have thought the same, but this was me, their friend. Or at least I thought I was. My heart dropped. Surgery? Have they always felt this way? Why would they have faked our friendship this long?

The pain of their words stung like a thousand bees and I didn't—I couldn't—listen anymore. I ran. I did not care where. I just wanted to get away from the hurt and betrayal. We'd been friends for years—to find out they were faking the entire time broke my heart. I would have done anything for them. Blinding sunlight hit my eyes as I escaped to my car. I peered out at the gray storm clouds rolling toward me and lost all control of my tears.

The shrill ring of a cell phone brought me back to the present. I pressed the stop button on the treadmill and answered without looking at the I.D. I knew it was my mother.

"Hi, Mom."

"Droplet, Are you ok?" My mom had the crazy belief it rained every time I cried. The year I was born still held the record for the most rainfall in the southeast. It's how I got the nickname.

At the sound of her motherly concern, my mind calmed. "I'm fine."

"If you are fine. why haven't I received a call since you girls moved? I know I have been working but a text would have eased a mother's mind."

"Shoot! I completely forgot."

"You forgot you hadn't spoken to your mother in three days?"

I rolled my eyes heavenward. "I am so sorry. We've just been really busy."

"What has you in your head so much it makes you forget your mother?"

"Nothing."

"Spill it. It has been raining, for goodness sake."

"Mom, just because it is raining doesn't mean there is something wrong. There is no scientific proof my emotions and the weather are tied in any way. Plus, it isn't raining here."

"True. But I know my daughter. Now, what is it? Is this about a boy?"

I sighed. "Fine, I'll tell you."

I proceeded to tell her what I'd overheard, conveniently leaving out my crying spell.

"Oh, those little bitches—"

"It's under control. Trust me.,"

Dr. Marilyn Blair was the best adoptive mother on the planet. The best heart surgeon in the region, she had worked at Phoenix Memorial for seven years.

"I love you, Droplet. I want you to know there isn't anything you can't talk to me about. I hate that you moved so far away, but I understand. You're a big girl. You don't need me anymore."

"Mom I'll always need you. You're a big girl too. You and Bill could use some alone time. Wink. Wink." I giggled. Bill was my mom's boyfriend. He was the first guy she'd dated since my dad passed from prostate cancer six years before. "But really, don't worry."

She sniffed. "It's a mother's job to worry." She paused for a moment. "Now you've kept me on the phone long enough. I have to go. I love you."

"I love you too."

Over the fireplace sat the first picture taken of me with my family. It was the day they adopted me. This was my only photo of them together. In Phoenix, I had taken down every picture of my father because Mom couldn't walk by them without crying. We could never be mistaken as blood relatives. Our differences were too great. Trent's skin was the color of refined chocolate. Where fair-skinned Mom has gunmetal-grey eyes that extract the truth from whoever is bold enough to look into them. Her willowy build was the complete opposite of my father's bodybuilder physique. *My freak show of a family,* I thought with affection.

In the photograph, I sat in Dad's arms, smiling at Trent. My fiery hair was wild and I wore a Minnie Mouse jumper. A silver bracelet with a large blue stone dangled from my tiny wrist. Tanzanite. That is what Dad called it. The bracelet was the inspiration of my favorite bedtime story.

I was found floating in the baptism pool of an old cathedral wearing nothing but that bracelet. Caretakers at the orphanage told my parents the bracelet was too small for them to slip over my wrist, but it wasn't hurting me, so there wasn't a problem. My parents thought it could be a clue to finding my birth mother when I got older. After bringing me home, my parents had a long talk on whether to remove it. The decision was to take it off and put it someplace safe.

I was greased down and soaped up in attempts to slide the adornment off. They even tried to cut it with tin snips, but the bracelet just would not budge. After two months, my parents had to return to work and I was off to daycare. One morning the bracelet and I were dropped off at daycare but that afternoon only one of us returned.

Dad was furious. Mom assumed it had finally popped off due to the damage Dad had done to it. No one at the daycare could remember a thing. (Safe to say I never went back to that facility.) Dad would make funny faces when he told the story. Each time, it was as if he was living it all over again.

Smiling, I set the photograph down on the mantel. Good thing I don't want to track my birth mother. She'd rejected me once and that was enough.

Maddie entered the house like a whirlwind, all blonde curls and long legs, wearing a pale pink mini frock and lace headband. She was super animated which was saying a lot for her. I could only catch every other word. There was something about a thrift store crawl, blah, blah, new Channing movie, blah, a fat dog in the road. She held up a brown puppy…"and now we have Oscar." She continued for a while as I listened from the couch. After a moment she stopped, staring at me.

"You alright?"

"Yes, just a bit sleepy."

"There's something else. What's going on?" Maddie was a person who could sense things you would rather keep to yourself. It was her only flaw.

"Nothing really. Just a bit antsy. I think I need to explore the city."

"I am so glad you said something. I have a date tonight and you're coming with."

"Let me think about it… No."

"But I need you there," she begged. "I don't know much about him. You can sit at the table all night if you want."

"Are you trying to lose your v-card?" I joked.

A strange look crossed her face. Guilt?

She winced. "Remember Blake Stevenson?"

"Stevenson? No. You did not!"

She threw an arm over her eyes. Yeah. She did.

"You let that guy deflower you?" I asked.

"Deflower?" she squeaked. "You really have to get your head out of those novels but yes. It's the biggest regret of my life. He was flopping on top of me like a fish." She frowned. "I'm not sure I like sex. I'm going to try it again to double check."

"In books, it is a magical thing. But based on my one experience, I have to agree with you. I don't think I want to do it again either. Where do authors get these beautiful stories?"

"Imagination, I guess. I think we had the wrong partners. Maybe we should interview them. You know. Hand out applications." We burst into a fit of laughter. "Seriously, you're next to get some lovin'."

I hit her with a silk throw pillow. "You're the one with the date tonight. Why don't you hush?"

She grabbed her purse and started digging. "Oh, I wanted to give you something."

She pulled out two matching boxes. One held a thin white-gold necklace with a tiny charm, a three-dimensional design of squiggly lines. In the other box, there was a necklace exactly like the first except it was yellow-gold. Removing them both, she interlocked the charms. The design formed the face of a woman with flowing hair.

"It is Philotes. She's the goddess of friendship. My mom helped me design it. She wanted me to give it to you for your birthday but I couldn't wait. What do you think? Do you like it?"

 "It's beautiful. I love it. Can I wear it now?"

"Yeah." We took turns fastening one another's necklaces.

I swiped at tears. "Okay, you've earned this night out."

"Great! But we are going in my car. You can drive just in case I really like my date. Your BMW is pretty but it is not environmentally safe."

"Your new wheels are pretty dope too."

"Thanks. It's a Mercedes C250. Dad had it modified to run on BIO fuel. It's what he calls a "get the hell out" gift. I call her EcoSwag," she grinned.

Club Sclavus was a three-story steamy box of sin. Muscle-shirt-wearing college guys crawled all over the place like ants. The girls wore skyscraper heels and little else. Inside, the walls glowed violet and pop art covered the bar. I was ready to leave as soon as we entered, but Maddie was using me as the backup plan. If her date stood her up or if it went horribly awry, I was there as support. We sat at a table closest to the dance floor waiting for her date to arrive.

Maddie yelled above the music pointing to some guy wearing a tight black shirt and an orange tan. "That guy sent you this." Glancing toward him, I lifted the drink as a thank you and smiled. *What is this? Drink number six? Wow. I must look really slutty.*

I was dressed in what Maddie calls "club attire," a super-shiny sea-foam high-neck mini-dress with black-lace side panels and peep toe black stilettos. The amount of makeup Madison had slathered on my face aged me at least five years. My hair was twisted up into a messy bun to show the black lace climbing up my neck. The hair pins were killing me. I was uncomfortable and completely out of my element. Plus, I looked like a hooker. Perfect. We hadn't even been carded.

"What time is your date coming?" I asked tugging on the hem of the dress.

"I don't know. He's twenty minutes late." I rolled my eyes. The guy was an idiot if he stood up a girl like Maddie. She was beautiful inside and out.

It must have been the drinks but I found myself wanting to dance. The deejay had me swaying in my seat. Maddie shook her head as some guy spoke in her ear. He gave her a pout and strolled to another girl.

"What did he want?" I asked when she turned back to face me.

"To dance."

"Why didn't you?"

She smiled. "I'm waiting on someone, remember?"

I laughed and walked onto the dance floor. The electric sounds of *Turn Up the Music* filled the room and I surrendered to the bass. Ripping out the torturous hair pins I released my imprisoned tresses and closed my eyes. Pure joy filled me as I moved to the rhythm. The subwoofers must have been on max because I could feel the pulse of the music resonating within my bones.

Another track. Another beat. The feel of strong arms didn't stop my motions. Soft lips breathed the lyrics of the song into my ear. His scent was intoxicating. Bergamot, I think.

Whoever this was could really move. Shifting precisely as I did.

"Please don't be orange tan guy," I thought, afraid of opening my eyes.

The dance continued. I breathed in. He breathed out. There were rumors about something called romantic chemistry but I hadn't believed in them until now. His arousal brushed against my hip. My breathing increased.

Ordinarily, this would have stopped or scared me but it didn't. For the first time in my life, I felt truly sexy.

I was aroused myself. Desire grew fast inside me. I was about to speak when the first drop hit. I glanced up just in time to see one, then another, sprinkler head begin spinning. I blinked and looked around the building. A circle had gathered around me and the mystery man. Maddie was in the front grinning ear-to-ear and gesturing me to turn around. She was practically jumping up and down. I frowned. Water rained down upon the crowd as I came face to face with eyes the color of melted gold.

It was not "orange tan guy" as I feared. It was much worse—I'd been dancing with what surely had to be a god. I stepped out of his arms. His eyes narrowed and his full lips tilted upward. The word "handsome" did not cut it. There was not an imperfection on this guy. His ebony hair fell an inch from muscular shoulders. Thick brows sat above eyes of gold. Sinful lips showed even white teeth in a smile that was downright predatory. His perfectly crafted features practically screamed to be caressed. I fisted my hands. Never in my wildest imagination could I have dreamt him up.

A hand jerked me away from the god pulling and tugging in the opposite direction. "Did you not see those flames?" Maddie scolded once we were safe by the car.

"Flames?" I repeated.

She shook her head, exasperated. "Look, let's go home. I'll drive. I'm pretty sure you're a little drunk but you have some serious moves. How come I've never seen them? I need to liquor you up more often. Wow! And that guy…"

"I know and I do have a bit of a buzz…"

"He sat watching you for almost six songs. Girls were offering to buy *him* drinks but he couldn't take his eyes off of you. I predict he is going to be your boyfriend."

"Oh shut up! I didn't even find out his name."

"What! You danced with him for two hours and you didn't ask his name?!"

I gaped at her. *Two hours?* "Is it always like that? The club?"

"No. Whatever you two had going on definitely was not a normal hook up."

"Sorry about your date."

"What do you mean? He was there. You didn't see him? Of course, you didn't. You were busy putting the moves on John Doe," she snickered. "Anyway, how are you so dry? Jealous. You were standing in the perfect spot. The sprinkler above you didn't come on, like you were in a bubble, just you and him. How romantic is that?"

I shrugged. Maddie was soaked. "Wonder what started the fire."

"Your dancing!" she chuckled.

"That guy..." I whispered. "He was... hot!" We burst into a crazy fit of laughter.

When we got home, I showered. While pulling on an over-size nightshirt, my thoughts flicker to those eyes. Maddie said we danced for two hours. How is that possible? I only remember three songs. It must have been the alcohol, but how drunk does a person have to be not to notice a fire? Beyonce's hit ran through my mind.

I grinned and slid into bed.

Dew on the windows acted as prisms reflecting streaks of color into my bedroom. I climbed out of bed and walked downstairs pulling on my robe. Maddie's room was the closest to the front door and I heard voices inside, so I decided against knocking and continued to the kitchen.

Fried fish and grits was my favorite breakfast. I put the grits into a pot to boil and cover the whiting in corn meal. Waiting on the oil to heat, I flipped on the television. The weatherman was talking about the long-lasting heat wave and adopting starving horses.

After finishing a couple of fillets, I heard Maddie and a male voice at the front door. Moments later she appeared in the kitchen, completely dressed in a body-hugging camisole in her signature pale pink with khaki bubble shorts and a stupid grin. She was radiant.

I turned to look at her. "Uhh…Okay? Good morning, Madison."

She smiled rocking back and forth on her heels. "Good morning, Gabriela," she said.

"What is it?"

"I had a visitor."

"I know. So, are you going to tell me who it was or not?"

"Yes. It was Mitchell."

"Who's Mitchell?"

She frowned. "The guy I met at the bar last night."

"Don't look at me like that. You never told me his name."

She skipped to the stove, piling enough food on her plate to feed a nation, and glanced at the TV. "Hey, look, they're talking about the fire at Club Sclavus!".

"The flames just appeared on the dance floor," a witness said.

"I'm just glad no one was hurt," said the owner.

A panned shot of the club surveyed the damage. The only thing left was a shell. "The fire department still does not know how or why the fire started," said the reporter. "If you have any information about what or who did this, please call the number at the bottom of your screen." I turned just in time to witness Maddie typing the number into her cell.

"You'd better not!" I screeched.

CYRUS

"Sire?"

I turned to face my second in command. "Yes, Teagan."

"Mistress Bianca is requesting an audience."

"Let her in," I grumbled. "And thanks."

"You're welcome." Teagan smirked and bowed.

The woman in question swept in without waiting for Teagan to announce her. He glared. I was sure if it hadn't been illegal to kill who he thought would be the future queen of the Phytian tribe, he would have snapped her pretty little neck right there.

I understood his need to kindly remove her head from her curvy little body, but she and I had been betrothed the day of her birth. It was touch and go for a while but she had grown into a gorgeous creature. She was raised as if she was guaranteed the crown and was spoiled rotten by the tribe.

My father chose her but after last night, he could unchoose her. It was not my fault I had found what few ever did.

Bianca waved her hand at me, pointing to where Teagan had exited. "You need better servants. I will arrange to hire a new second for you this week. I swear I do not know how you have put up with that brute."

"Hello to you too, Bianca," I said. "And no, you aren't arranging anything for my court. I will have no more talking about Teagan in such a disrespectful manner. You forget yourself. He could disembowel you in a blink and you would not notice until you woke at the pearly gates.

"We are not bonded nor are you my moiety. Killing you is not illegal for him and from the glint in his eye when you are around, I think it is best for you to back off. Considering your unannounced visits to my home, I may allow it. You know I handle all Phytian matters within the royal residence. So why are you here?"

Bianca frowned, ignoring the question. "You would never allow him to murder your fiancée."

"You are not my fiancée. We are *betrothed*. Fiancée implies I had some kind of choice. Murdox picked you, not me."

She flinched but rebounded quickly. "Your father chose me because I have the best breeding. I am Phytian through and through. I am the pinnacle of the bloodlines after the royal family. I eat, speak, stand, and walk better than any other in our tribe. I am also more educated and cultured than anyone else, but you refuse to see these facts. Others would kill to have me at their side."

I rolled my eyes. "Well, they are permitted to have you and listen to your little speeches. I'll ask again. Why are you here?"

"When you start realizing how fortunate you are I will stop giving these little speeches. I will be your queen someday and I will not stand for being second to Teagan or your whores."

Ah, I thought, *now we are getting to the point of this visit.* I didn't bother to correct her about her demotion of status. Telling her now would only serve to make her suicidal...or homicidal. I didn't want to find out which.

Bianca stared at me. "I mean it, Cyrus. Do something about your whore fan club. You sleep with all these humans and mix-breeds but won't touch your future wife. It's embarrassing. You act as if sleeping with mutts is gratifying."

"That is enough! Go home!"

She started to respond, but I held up my hand. "No, don't speak. Just leave. Please. And don't come back to my home again without an invitation."

She huffed, and turned her back to me. As she reached the door, it opened to reveal Teagan standing just outside. As she swept out, he formed a small flame and tossed it at her feet. She shrieked before smothering the fire with her own flame and looking at her shoes, now smoking. "These are Brian Atwoods," she said as she glared at him.

He grinned. "They were."

Hissing, Bianca stomped away.

Teagan and I frowned at the same time. "What are Atwoods?" Teagan shrugged.

Teagan is not only my second but one of my best friends. We grew up in training camp together and formed a bond that was legendary. He is more my brother than a friend.

Teagan grinned. "It was the least she deserved after trying to get me fired. So…when are you going to tell her? Can I be there?"

"Tell her what?"

"About your moiety. You forget Niko and I were there. We witnessed the woman's aura flash the moment you touched her. She is yours."

"I don't know. I know nothing about her. I need to court her. She oozes innocence."

"Wow!! Really? Virginal innocence or inexperience innocence?"

"The latter. The look in her eyes said she had a few ideas." I stopped. "Damn. I know I don't have to tell you to keep this quiet…but please do. For some reason, I feel I have to hide her right now—especially from Murdox and Bianca."

"I understand. What about your mother?"

I thought for a moment. "I will tell her at the fundraiser."

"Good deal," said Teagan. "I'll see you tomorrow night."

Although I was doing everything in my power to find the Enchantress, I didn't want others involved in the hunt, and I would not allow anyone other than Teagan and Niko to even know about her. It would be hard. Although Ocean Peak wasn't a rural town, it was rare for someone who looked like her to go unnoticed.

I was about to leave Sclavus when I saw her. Finding a chair closer to the floor, I sat and watched as she moved her lithe little body. She was exquisite. Her bronze skin glowed in the darkness of the club. She had legs that started at her armpits and eyes of the most startling green. Those eyes...I saw the heat in them the moment she turned to me.

After a moment, a kind of panic entered those emerald orbs. Innocence bled from her and it was in that moment I knew. She belonged to me. With me.

There were few places a person could go to party on the island but a couple of gems lay hidden for locals—Sclavus and Moist. I guessed that she was a local resident or a friend of one. Sclavus was not a place tourists visited. Moist was the only option.

The fundraiser was boring as usual. I only attended because my mother, Amaryl, would have had a conniption if I'd chosen not to show. Amaryl was the most important woman in my life. I would have taken a bullet before disappointing her in any way. She was kindness and love at its zenith, and though she had few, if any, tribal powers, she could hold her own. You had to have thick skin when you were moiety to one of the most ruthless men in history.

"Dedi," said Amaryl.

"Mother." I kissed her on the cheek.

"Glad to see you could make it." Her eyes twinkled—she'd known I would come. "No date tonight?"

"Actually, that is what I wanted to speak with you about. Can we speak privately?"

She steered me to a corner of the balcony. "Yes?"

Getting as close to her ear without appearing too secretive, I told her what I'd found. She inhaled half the oxygen in the room before showing a brittle smile.

Her response caught me off guard. "I thought you would be happy."

She attempted a smile again. "I am. It is only that I'm concerned for you. You said you have never seen her at any rally. How could that be? All must attend."

"Thousands show for those things, Amaryl."

"Of course. However, I think we should keep this between the two of us until you find her. When you do, bring her to me. I would like to meet the female who will take my place someday." Her eyes sparked in quiet determination. "There is a purpose for the things we do. I love you, Cyrus."

"I know, Mother, and I love you."

A comfortable silence fell over both of us as we looked around the room. A red-haired vixen who'd done everything to gain my attention dropped a flute of champagne and made a show of bending over to pick up its broken pieces without using her knees.

My mother stiffened. She'd seen it too.

She spoke without looking at me. "Your doting fans follow you everywhere. Now that you are soon to be bonded, you will regret having lain with women like that."

"I already do."

For the first time, she chuckled. "How hearts will break when they hear the news."

***

Niko Targolski still could not believe what he'd witnessed. His friend, his brother, the prince had fallen head over heels at first sight with a stranger. It had been appalling enough when Teagan made a fool of himself when meeting his Phoebe. This was Cyrus, playboy and future king.

Now, the three of them had been searching for the girl for days. A human girl! No. Not *completely* human, but close enough that her aura was almost non-existent. It was freaky. The connection between them hadn't been the slow building of aural energy as it had been with Phoebe. Instead, it had been an explosion.

"Hello-o-o." Niko blinked to find Teagan's hand an inch from his face.

"Oh-h-h." Teagan doubled over feigning agony.

"Shut up. I didn't hit you hard."

Teagan stood up. The grin on his face confirmed Niko's suspicions.

"What! You can't take a joke, Niko?"

"I won't let you sucker punch me twice."

"Come on. That was years ago! Stop holding that over my head. What were you thinking about anyway? And don't tell me it was nothing."

"I can have some thoughts to myself."

"Not from your brothers. I could have been an assassin."

"You're not my *real* brother."

The oldest of the trio, Niko joined the group after Teagan and Cyrus were already well bonded, but somehow he had managed to worm his way into their circle. And then, after each of them had had near death experiences in the horrible camps, they'd begun to consider themselves brothers. Truth was Niko thought they were more blood to him than anyone other except his mother.

Teagan made a face. "We may not be birthed from the same womb, but you're my brother. Now answer my fucking question or I *will* sucker punch you."

Niko cleared his throat and told Teagan about his worry at Cyrus's having fallen in love with a near-human.

Teagan tried to reassure him. "But you've only seen one true moiety shift right? And like you said it was only a flash."

Mitchell chuckled. "I'd pay to see that again."

Maddie laughed too. "The last time I saw you dance like that, you were drunk. If you become one of those alcoholics, I'll move out."

"If you move out I'll become one of those alcoholics," I joked, still embarrassed.

"So you had a party?"

I rolled my eyes and Maddie stuck out her tongue. "We were in the TV room. The note was from *this morning*." She emphasized the last two words. "It's not morning anymore."

Hector cleared his throat. "You look good. It's very 1920s," he mused, his eyes roving over my night-gown-clad form.

"Thanks. Nice to see you too," I said without a hint of embarrassment. He smiled as I went to my room to change.

Everyone sat around the flat screen when I returned. Maddie and Mitchell were cuddling at one end of the sofa. One eating up whatever the other whispered, like M&M's. I ran to Hector, flopped down on his lap to give him the noisiest kiss on the cheek I could make.

Hector grinned. He was the best gal pal a girl could have—tall, dark, handsome and extremely gay. Maddie and I met him on a family vacation before Dad died. He was visiting his grandparents who lived across the street. We all had been pen pals ever since.

"Hey guys!" said Maddie. "Mitchell wants to go dancing. You in?"

Hector winked. "I'm game. I would love to see Droplet cut a rug again."

I shrugged. "Sure."

Maddie squealed her excitement.

Forty-five minutes later, I was standing in the mirror once again amazed at Maddie's skills. She really should become a stylist. The black off-the-shoulder sequined midi-dress, adorned with gold accessories and shoes, gave my body grace and elegance. Soft waves fell over my shoulders and my makeup was natural this time. I felt like myself...but hot.

"Do you like it?" Maddie asked.

"You are an artist."

"I just polished a diamond," she said.

"You look great as always." She wore a hot pink bandage dress with a sweetheart neckline and white stilettos. Her locks were neatly pinned into a complex up-do.

"Thanks," she said, making a face. "I have some bad news. Hector isn't coming. He has to work early tomorrow but Mitchell's brother Rhett is going instead."

"Well, that sucks about Hector. I really wanted to meet his boyfriend."

"Me too."

A car horn blared. Grabbing our bags, we locked up and walked to the car. The guys held open a door for each of us. Their faces were priceless. It took immense self-control not to tip Mitchell's chin up to close his mouth.

"Beautiful," he whispered as Maddie brushed by him. He gave her the most sexual smile. I had to look away.

"I'm going to make some guys jealous tonight myself," said the new guy, Rhett.

I gave him a shy smile and slid into the car. "Thanks. I'm Gabriela and you don't look bad yourself."

Mitchell and Rhett weren't real brothers but fraternity. You wouldn't have known by looking at them. They were the same height, same build and dressed alike.

When we drove into the parking lot, people were lined up against the brick exterior of Club Moist. We didn't get in line but went straight to the door. The doorman handed us armbands and pulled Rhett aside. Mitchell stopped to buy a pitcher of cranberry and vodka at the bar while Maddie and I found a table closest to the dance floor.

Green and blue strobe lights pulsed with every drum kick. I swayed to the music while we talked and watched the crowd. Rhett sat close to me. Our conversation veered to relationship status.

"Excuse me." We all turned to see a gorgeous waitress with a bright green drink.

"For you," she said, handing me the glass.

I lifted a brow. "What is it?"

"Um… It's called The Green-Eyed Monster." She smirked and walked away.

"Oh! That's bold." I pulled Maddie to her feet. "Excuse us, gentlemen. We have to powder our noses."

Leaving the restroom, Maddie noticed a familiar face in the hall. "Hi. Jennifer, right?" she asked.

"Yeah. I thought that was you guys," said Jennifer with a smile that didn't quite reach her eyes.

"You should sit with us," Maddie said, suddenly frowning. "That is, if we can remember where we sat."

"I know where you were. I'll show you," said the girl. This time her smile was genuine.

We followed Jennifer through a narrow corridor. A large group of girls was watching another vomit violently.

There was no way we were going to get past without trouble. Jennifer led us to another hall. There was only a couple making out in this one. They were all tongues and hair pulling.

"Olivia," said Jennifer slyly, "have you met Mitchell's girlfriend, Madison?" The couple slowly pulled apart, both breathing like they'd just finished a triathlon. Maddie and I were shocked the other half of the writhing mass was Rhett.

Olivia was a drop dead beauty. Her curvaceous body was packaged in a baby blue freak 'em dress. There was more skin showing than dress but she wore it well. "Hi. It's good to see Mitchell with someone," she said with a warm smile.

Maddie and I just gaped. Go Rhett.

"Um… are you okay?" Olivia asked.

"I'm sorry. I'm Gabriela–I met Rhett tonight."

"I'm Olivia." She gestured to Rhett with her head. "Well, *I've* met him before. He's my boyfriend." Maddie still hadn't said a word.

Jennifer had a look of satisfaction on her face. I smiled at her genuinely and she frowned. "I will meet you back at the table, Liv," she said.

"Okay," responded Olivia, giving Maddie a strange look.

I poked Maddie. "We better get going. I know Mitchell is lonely by now." I nodded toward Olivia. "Nice meeting you."

I weaved an arm through one of Maddie's and pulled her back to the table. There was a new pitcher of cranberry and vodka. Maddie glared at Mitchell. "Did you know!?" she yelled over the music.

"Know what?"

"You know damn well what! Rhett and Olivia! I was going to hook him up with Gabby."

I swung my head around to look at Maddie. "What?! I do not want to be with anyone and no offense, but definitely not Rhett."

"Are you ready to leave?" Maddie had suddenly become all huffy.

I shook my head. "No. I'm going to dance. Seriously there was nothing there. You should have told me."

"You would have said no," she said, pouting. "And I don't want to dance."

The floor wasn't crowded and I swayed to the music as the deejay mixed a few techno tracks. Florence Welch started to serenade the first line of Cosmic Love while lasers pulsed every color. My body moved to the tunes of my favorite band and I was lost. There was only me and the music. Numbing euphoria swept through me. My breathing grew loud in my ears and my heart began to pound.

The song morphed into Blinding. As the music intensified so did my confidence. The alcohol was beginning to take effect. My feet shifted as if preprogrammed and my hands swirled imaginary patterns above my head. Seven Devils thundered over the crowd and I fell deeper into the trance. Heat enveloped me and the mouthwatering scent of bergamot filled the air. I inhaled deeply, rocking my shoulders and twirling my hips.

My trance was lifted when a feeling of paranoia crawled down my spine. I opened my eyes and my heart nearly stopped. Sitting in a chair right in the middle of the dance floor was the mystery man from Club Sclavus. His golden gaze was scorching and I knew the look would haunt my dreams forever.

Something deep within my soul stirred and reached for him. Panic began to rise in my chest and I took a step back.

When I did, he stood. He wore a fitted gray shirt, dark jeans, and had one hell of an erection. His fiery golden eyes were practically stripping clothing from my body.

I took another step back, prepared to run. His eyes narrowed and a corner of his mouth quirked upward. "Keep dancing for me."

I froze. I hadn't been dancing for him. Had I?

"Or with me."

I was frightened of him but I longed to be in his arms again. Nervousness made my motions awkward but soon my muscles relaxed and I stepped toward him. Our movements were synchronized as we stared into each other's eyes. Tight against him, I could feel the thump of his heart against mine. His body swayed and rocked demanding mine to answer. The combination of alcohol and lasers emboldened me. I raised my hand to his face and stroked his jawline. He closed his eyes but he didn't stop moving. Realizing what I had done, I pulled my hand away and he opened his eyes again. Their color appeared different, darker.

"What's your name?" I whispered, in a soft breathy purr. *Was that my voice?*

"Cyrus Zorn. Yours?" His voice was deep and gravelly.

"Gabriela Blair."

"You are an empirical beauty, Gabriela. You have cast some sort of spell on me. I just knew your name was Enchantress or Witch."

I laughed. "If that's a line, consider me hooked."

"My beautiful witch. Ever since I laid eyes on you all I can think about is how it is going to be when I take you." He spun me around to face the crowd.

I arched my back. "When you take me?"

"Yes, I can almost smell the lust coming off of you. I am throwing off enough heat to cause a fire myself. One way or another, we will be together." He growled it like a threat.

Goosebumps caused me to shiver. I could not deny whatever was happening between us. I took a shaky breath. He chuckled. "Tell me your phone number. I want to see you somewhere quiet."

I recited the digits as we continued to move as one. He held me close for a long while and for the first time, I felt safe. The song morphed into another. This one more upbeat. His arms loosened and I spun to face him, but he was gone. Vanished.

Weaving through the throng of people I saw no sign of him and finally gave up. I made my way back to the table. Maddie and Mitchell were on the edge of the floor dancing. I'd never seen Maddie so happy.

"Excuse me, again," said the brunette waitress from earlier. This time she held a white drink. "It's called Enchantress."

Smiling, I thanked her, and Maddie plopped down next to me.

"John Doe put that smile there?" She shook her head. "I mean, really. You two have a connection I do not understand. It is so intense, you know?"

My smile changed to a full on grin.

Mitchell sat next to Maddie. They made sickening goo-goo eyes at each other.

"You ladies ready to go?" Mitchell asked.

I nodded but Maddie shook her head.

"You guys stay. I'll call an uber."

"Absolutely not! We're going. We came together. We leave that way," Maddie said, now looking for her purse.

I bent over to retrieve my own and a sharp pain on my hip caused me to stand and spin.

"Nice ass!" an orange moron slurred.

Maddie was in his face before his words registered. "What the hell do you think you are doing?" Mitchell pulled her behind him.

Smart move. The orange idiot was almost twice Mitchell's size, but it didn't stop him from squaring his shoulders and glaring at the guy.

"You've got a nice piece of pussy there. A bit temperamental for my taste, but I bet she's a nice fuck. It is not fair for you to have two. I'll take this one and you can keep the she-wolf." He reached out toward me.

In a heartbeat, Cyrus stood between the two men. His sudden reappearance took my breath away. No words were spoken but the guy paled, his skin changing from rust to a sickly cream-sickle orange. "I didn't know she was with anyone," he sputtered, raising his hands and backing away. Cyrus turned and nodded before merging into the crowd once more.

Back home Maddie followed me to my bedroom only to state the obvious.

"He was watching you again."

"I figured as much."

"Did you find out his name? Did you get his number?"

"Yes and no. His name is Cyrus."

"No? Why on earth didn't you get his number?"

"Didn't ask for it. I gave him mine."

She rolled her eyes. "Now we have to wait for him to call you. Ugh!"

A smile returned to her face. "Mitchell is staying over tonight and we're going out for breakfast in the morning. We will bring you something back."

"Thanks. You are the best."

"Don't I know it." She winked as she closed the door behind her.

GABRIELA

After a day without a phone call from Cyrus, I'd given up. I would not sit around like a newly-trained puppy.

It was my day to cook and it felt like a pancake kind of morning. I gathered all my supplies and noticed there was no maple syrup in the fridge. Checking the pantry, I saw thin threads shimmering seconds before I came face to face with a grizzly-bear-sized spider. I screamed. Maddie was beside me in seconds. Oscar barked his concern.

"What's wrong?" asked Maddie.

"I should ask *you* that. Are you allergic to something? Your lips are swollen."

She laughed so hard I began to think I should call 911.

"I'll explain later. What were you screaming about?"

I pointed to the spider and she doubled over again. "Don't laugh at me. You know I hate those things."

Mitchell entered the kitchen pulling a shirt over his head. "What is it?" he asked.

Maddie pointed at the spider. Mitchell laughed. "For goodness sake! We thought someone was trying to kill you." He grabbed a paper towel and did away with the spider.

Everyone jumped when my cell rang. Racing across the kitchen, I answered without a glance at the ID.

"Hi. This is Cyrus."

"Um... Hi. I mean Good Morning." I pumped my fist in Maddie's direction.

"If you don't have anything to do today I would love to spend some time with you. Or we can just go out for coffee."

"I'm free," I said and gave him the address.

"Great! I'll be there at twelve. See you then."

The doorbell rang at exactly twelve. I took a deep breath and opened the door. Cyrus stood holding two large canvas bags.

"Hi. What's all this?" I asked, grabbing one.

"We are going to pig out and watch some of the best movies ever made."

I waved him through the door. "Sounds like fun. Do these best movies ever made have names?" I hoped against hope there were no slashers.

"Well," he proclaimed with the excitement of a nine-year-old. "The best one is the 1990's hit Teenage Mutant Ninja Turtles."

"How did you know my favorite movie? I'm a Ralph-a-holic."

"Good guess." He moved around the kitchen with ease and opened the refrigerator. He eyed a large bowl of vegan gummy bears and raised an eyebrow.

I giggled. "They're Maddie's."

Cyrus opened a cupboard and glanced back. "Your friend from the bar?"

"Yeah. She is my heart. What are you cooking?"

"I will be preparing a vegan—"

"Vegan?! Not you too! Can I have some real food for once?" I said before I could stop myself. I tried to apologize with my eyes. "I'm so sorry. I didn't mean to—"

He laughed. "It's okay. I thought you were a health nut. I'm not a vegan either."

I shivered. "Good. Maddie makes some of the most disgusting things."

He closed the cupboard. "We can pig out on homemade pizza later then."

Without a word he gathered me into his arms and carried me to the den. It felt like we had done this a million times.

Thirty minutes into the movie, Cobain's voice blared from Cyrus' cell. He rolled his eyes and answered. "I'm busy." He listened for a moment to the voice on the other end and then frowned. "What? You have got to be kidding me... Now?"

He hung up without a goodbye and turned to me. "I'm sorry, but I have to go," he said in a much softer tone. "There's a family emergency. Please allow me to take a rain check."

"Sure," I said. "Don't worry about it. I hope everything is all right."

"I'll call you when I can."

I barely made it to see him pull out of the driveway before locking the door. After wandering around in the house, I decided to take a shower. I'd barely gotten the water on when I heard noises coming from my bedroom. The door to the bathroom opened. It was Hector. "Gabriela?"

I peeked through the door of the shower and rolled my eyes. He was standing there with our puppy Oscar in his arms. "Get out and take that crazed animal with you," I said.

Hector whined. "What did Oscar ever do to you?

I smirked. "I was talking to Oscar. I'm showering if you didn't notice."

"I can see that."

"Hector if you don't get out I am going to happily beat you to death!" I threatened.

"Look I'm gay but I'm still male. I can appreciate women's jiggly bits just like any other guy." He sounded completely confident.

I screeched.

A loud clank was the only warning before the shower head tilted and water arched over the door. Hector let out a high-pitched shriek and ran into my bedroom. Oscar followed in his wake, shaking the water out of his fur.

I stepped out of the shower. Wrapping a towel around me, I walked into the bedroom. Hector was sitting on the bed with Oscar beside him. "What was so important that you had to barge in on me in the shower?"

"Your mom called and asked me to check on her droplet. She was convinced that you didn't sound well this morning. Apparently, she called Maddie and she didn't answer, so you were graced with my presence." He grinned and whistled. "I can see you're okay so I'll pass on that to your mom. Where's Madison anyway?"

"I didn't have time to talk to her because I had a date. And Maddie is with Mitchell somewhere."

"Hold on. Did you say *date*?"

"Yeah, but we can talk about that later. Help me catch Oscar and dry him off."

"Can't. Avery is waiting in the car. Love ya." He blew a kiss as he ran to the door.

"You get back here and help me," I yelled, only to hear the front door slam shut.

***

Two days passed before Cyrus called again. This time he instructed me to be up and dressed comfortably by 9 a.m.

At the stroke of nine, the doorbell rang. "Ready to go?" he asked. I nodded. I was about to close the door behind us when Maddie, the shrew, flounced down the stairs. I hadn't told her about seeing Cyrus again. My love life— or lack of one—was never on my mind when Maddie and I were together. I didn't want her to know I was going to see Cyrus again. I didn't want to get her hopes up if this didn't work out.

Despite my attempt, the door opened behind us and Maddie stood looking him up and down. "Why, hello there. You must be Cyrus."

I groaned.

Cyrus nodded and grinned. "Yes. And you are the famous Madison." That earned him a smile.

"Where are you two off to this early?"

"It's a secret."

"Figures. We only saw you at night so I attributed your good looks to mystery, you know? Like Dracula. You kind of reek of the sexy, brooding, dangerous, night creature. The newer Vlad—not the original." She gazed at him for a moment. "But you're pretty hot in the daylight too."

I smiled at her, but my eyes told a different story. "Maddie, my sweet friend, we have to get going."

"Fine," she said, glaring back, "but you and I will talk."

Cyrus chuckled as we climbed into my car. He had ridden his bike over and tucked it inside the garage. "She's interesting," he said. You don't know the half of it, I thought.

I punched the directions Cyrus gave me into my GPS and we were off. We talked as we drove. We were about five miles from any part of civilization. Dirt roads and tracks had taken us to a densely wooded area and into a forest. Just the perfect place for a villain sighting. Jason. Michael. Big Foot. Then the trees began to thin out and a tiny circular clearing opened before us.

"Pull over here," Cyrus instructed.

There is no way I'm getting out of this car, I thought. Hottie or no hottie, animals sat in wait to devour us.

When I didn't say anything, Cyrus grinned. "Aw, come on. Don't you trust me?"

"Not this much," I answered without hesitation.

"Can you try to?"

I put the car in park and scrutinized him. He reached for his backpack. "Come on. I promise to protect you."

"You don't mess with the Sasquatch. Haven't you watched the commercials?"

After a second, Cyrus opened my door and pulled me gently out of the car.

The wilderness is totally not my thing. I would rather curl up on the sofa with a best seller and a bag of Skittles. Cyrus practically drug me up hills and actually picked me up and carried me over muddy areas.

"Where are we going? Hogwarts?" I asked.

"Shhh…" he said, as we came to a stop in front of a colossal oak tree that looked to be over a thousand years old. Its bottom branches had grown so heavy they brushed the forest floor. I was suddenly giddy. Climbing this tree was a must.

I turned to Cyrus but he had ninja-vanished. "Cyrus?"

"Shhh…Up here. Come on," he whispered. He'd already climbed up most of the tree.

Thank goodness for shoe traction. I made it to him and we found a sturdy fork to sit on high in the canopy. Cyrus dug an umbrella out of his bag and opened it with a pop. Rustling leaves broke the silence as squirrels played and birds chirped a song in the distance. The notes were lovely as the song swelled in volume.

We watched as a multi-colored bird landed one branch below us. It too joined the chorus. This feathered creature was dazzling, almost as if it had been dipped in one of God's most beautiful rainbows. I reached out only to have it fly away, but I didn't have to wait long before another perched on a limb next to us.

Eyes wide, I slowly ran my finger over its wing, and in what seemed an instant, there were thousands of the rainbow birds surrounding us. A kaleidoscope of color above and below. The beauty of their tune nearly brought me to tears.

"What are they?" I whispered, not wanting to startle them.

Cyrus whispered back. "Painted Buntings. I've read they are rare but I don't think scientists know anything about this place. I think they come here to find their mate."

"How did you find it?"

Cyrus smiled. "Wandering."

"Wow."

I don't know how long we sat before Cyrus suggested we climb down. The birdsong ended long before and most of the painted buntings were gone.

Once safely on the ground, we walked hand in hand to the car. I watched as Cyrus wrapped the umbrella in a plastic sleeve he retrieved from his backpack.

"The idea for the umbrella was brilliant. The buntings were incredible. Thank you for bringing me," I said.

"Thank you for coming."

On the way back, Cyrus received another urgent call on his cell. At home, he stared deep into my eyes, building my anticipation for a kiss, only to plant it on my cheek. I was disappointed but I smiled and watched him speed away again.

Maddie threw the door open. "Bad date? Where did you go? Why didn't you tell me? How come Hector knew before I did?"

Maddie continued to fire questions at me and I rolled my eyes heavenward. "Look, I didn't try to hide it from you. I was going to tell you but I didn't think about it when we were together. This has not been going on long, so relax. And before you ask again, I was upset because so far, he hasn't kissed me." When I saw her surprise, I confessed. "Yes, I really want him to."

The sound of her laughter followed me up the stairs.

CYRUS

I reported on the date to Teagan. "Your plan worked like a charm. She was pissed. She was absolutely livid."

Teagan grinned. "I told you. Nothing makes a girl think more than *not* getting a kiss when you have given her an unbelievable date. That was a trick my father taught me. I got my Phoebe out of that advice."

I thought for a moment. "Phoebe *is* a gem."

"I know it," Teagan said with pride.

Teagan was the last of the Phytians to actually find his moiety, after my father and mother.

I thought about Gabriela. "So, what do you think? I should make my move on the next date?"

"I don't know my friend. She doesn't appear ready to submit."

A sultry female voice interrupted our planning session. It was Teagan's nemesis, Bianca. "I am totally ready to submit. I was measured for my crown last year. I was thinking a tiara, but after talking to my stylist we thought a crown would fit my personality better. Besides, your father okayed it as long as it is smaller than yours." She strode into the room.

Teagan muttered under his breath. "No doubt it will be. So small it will be invisible.

I coughed, trying not to laugh, and then raised my head and glared at her. "Hello, Bianca. What brings you to my home on this fine day…without an invite as usual?"

She smirked at me. "Well, since you asked so nicely, it was your hoard of groupies. I have been accosted about you not taking new lovers to your bed." She eyed me speculatively. "Why is that? Are you ready for my submission?"

"No."

"No?" She parroted, surprised.

"I will not accept your submission. You are not my moiety."

"Why on earth do you keep bringing that up? Over the last fifty years, only four have found their true mates."

Bianca shook her head at me. "You must come out of this dream, darling. Your father only wants the best for you and I am it."

Teagan snorted. "You will never be anyone's mate because you are selfish. You more than anyone should fear the joining. You are too shortsighted to understand the meaning of a ceremony so sacred. Do you even know what it means?"

I was a little nervous. I knew Teagan would never tell Bianca about Gabriela, but I also knew he would enjoy making her look like a fool.

She glowered at him. "Of course, I do. It is a ceremony where a female sexually submits to her mate in order to accept him. If he is found unsuitable, she does not submit. If she rejects his advances for a year, he is rendered both sterile and impotent. Once done it cannot be undone." She rattled off the words like she was taking an oral exam.

"Ha! Your robotic reply proves your lack of understanding. A mate's submission is not only sexual—she does it with her entire being. Phoebe and I made love

80

many times before she gave everything she was and will be into my keeping."

My lieutenant's last words were said with such possession and pride that Bianca took a step back as he continued. He shook himself and breathed deeply. "A male will do any and everything he can to get her to accept him. He feels a need, a hunger, a drive to claim what is his, so no other fucker dares to touch her. It is a bond you cannot be taught in a classroom or by a tutor. It is elemental. No, the act of sex itself is not enough to trigger the binding of souls."

Bianca turned to me with a pout. "I will be going now. You have allowed your beast of a guard to insult enough of my sensibilities for one day with his crass language and boorish behavior. I just came to make sure you were healthy and I can see that you are."

Just as she disappeared through the door, Teagan threw flames toward her feet. "Dude. I fucking hate her. I know I should feel sorry for her but she makes that shit impossible. Did you hear her? 'She has to sexually submit,'" he mimicked. "Who taught her that? You should fire them."

I laughed at his seriousness. "Forget about Bianca and tell me the next step in the plan with Gabriela."

The following day I put Teagan's plan into action. I called Gabriela and asked her to be ready for dinner around seven. Then I called a stylist—there would be no half-stepping for me tonight—I wanted it to be perfect for her. I'd made reservations at Shades, the best restaurant on the island. My black Audi Roadster was freshly washed and ready to go.

I rang the bell at exactly seven. When the door opened, the sight before me was what fairy tales are written about. A short red dress with a cape hugging her shoulders. Tall black spiked pumps showed her shapely legs off to perfection. Her jet black tresses hung in waves around a face so angelic it was heartbreaking. The pet name I had given her fit more perfectly with every meeting. She was a witch, casting enchantment spells every time I was close to her.

"Wow," I gulped. "You look..." I couldn't find the right word.

A pretty pink flush bloomed under her bronze skin. "Thanks. You look amazing yourself," she whispered.

"Thank you. Ready to go?"

"Yes."

The small elegant restaurant created quite a romantic atmosphere with its dark gray walls and soft candle light. Beautiful red amaryllis sat at each table. Smooth jazz played on an old jukebox near a semi-crowded dance floor.

We talked about music, movies, but mostly our dreams for the future. I was not shocked when she told me about her hidden passion for dance. "Your body should always be in motion," I said.

I noticed every little nuance when she answered a question. She had a nervous tell of rubbing her thumb over each fingertip on her left hand when she was uncomfortable with a question. Whenever she smiled it was genuine, turning her bright eyes into thin lines of sunshine. Her laugh was full and sultry.

She told me a few things about her mom, brother, Madison and even her father, whom she had told me earlier had passed away. "He is my best friend. Words can't describe how much I miss him."

I touched her hand. "You said he *is* your best friend, not was."

"I know. I don't believe just because I can't see him it means he is gone. Was is past tense and there is nothing past about his impact on my life. He is a part of me and as long as I live, so shall he."

I slid closer to her. A need to wrap my arms around her drove me hard. My eyes fell to her lips and I leaned over and placed mine on her's. In my mind, I heard a sweet voice whisper, "Great to see you again," but fire roared through me and I knew I was a goner. All I felt, smelled and tasted was Gabriela. My body, mind, and spirit dancing with hers in that moment. She melted into me and it took all my self-control not to take her there in the restaurant.

"Wow. You never kissed me like that," said the voice, this time so whiny and childlike it snapped me out of my thoughts. I pulled away and glared at the intruder. Rachel was what my mother called one of my fan club hussies. She was one of the most beautiful women in the world but she could not compare to my witch. Her skin was the color of the purest milk chocolate with eyes to match. Her mile-long legs were enough to make the highest-paid model take a hit to her self-esteem.

"Here I am trying to kiss my date and you just have to butt in."

"Don't you miss me, Cy?" Whined Rachel.

"No, Rachel, I don't. I am in the middle of something here if you haven't noticed."

"I see," she retorted. "Call me when you are tired of hanging in the slums."

Gabriela watched as she sauntered away. "Did you hear her before you kissed me?"

I looked at her in confusion.

"Did you hear her call your name before you kissed me?"

I was irritated at the whole situation. "I don't see how that matters."

Gabriela grabbed her purse and stood up. "Thank you for a nice time. I would like to go home now."

"You want to leave?"

"Yes. Now, please."

I dropped a couple hundred on the table and followed her to the car. I was about to put the key in the ignition but stopped. "Gabriela, tell me what I did wrong."

"Just take me home."

"Tell me first, and I swear I will."

"Fine. I don't appreciate the 'fuck you' kiss in front of your ex."

"What?"

"You would not have kissed me if she hadn't been there."

"I kissed you because there was nothing on this planet more important to me."

"You knew she was there and you wanted to hurt her. You embarrassed her. You kissed me right in front of the poor girl. And like that, no less."

"Did Rachel look embarrassed to you? If the president of the United States had been there trying to gain my attention he too would have had to wait. Nothing short of the world ending that exact moment was going to stop me from kissing you. Like nothing will stop this one," I declared, reaching over to pull her onto my lap.

The kiss was soft at first but built in intensity. Her licks, nips, and tugs were almost my undoing. For a moment we were lost, feasting on each other. She groaned low in her throat. I pulled away with a feeling of crazed possession.

"Your place or mine?" I said between breaths.

"Mine," she breathed and slid back into her seat. I loved that she didn't pretend not to know what I was talking about.

I weaved in and out of traffic fast enough to impress Dale Earnhardt. We'd barely made it inside the house before I was holding her firmly against a wall for our third life-altering kiss. "Ask me."

"Ask you what?"

"Ask me to make love to you. Ask me to be inside of you. To become one with you. You were upset about the kiss at the restaurant. I will not offend you again. So ask me, my witch."

"Please," she whimpered.

We were in her bedroom in a matter of seconds. I laid her on the bed like a precious gift and ripped my shirt over my head. I lazily unzipped my slacks while staring at her like a predator. If I had not been in such a hurry to get inside of her, I would have stood there and let her continue to eye-fuck me.

Her arousal scented the room, which caused me to salivate. I felt the change in her the moment a sliver of moonlight revealed the scars marring my skin. Her scent grew stronger as she ran her thumb over her fingertips. I knew she was mine.

The urge to claim and own burned deep inside. I saw her stiffen and felt a smirk cross my face. I pushed my pants to the floor and she moaned.

"Shh...I've got you," I said, as gently as I could.

I slowly removed her clothing and felt shivers shake her body while heat radiated from my own. I licked the sweet little arch of her neck as my fingers pressed firmly against her spine and she moaned louder. I snaked an arm between her thighs and applied pressure where I knew she needed it most. Pushing two fingers into her wet heat, I pumped them slowly in and out.

"Gabriela, open your eyes. See me," I demanded, removing my hand and giving my fingers a lingering lick. I groaned at my first taste of her and watched her eyes as I forced her thighs wider. My mouth continued its leisurely exploration—soon replacing my fingers—and I lightly teased her folds, ratcheting up her need for me. When she was on the cusp, I stopped. She groaned her frustration and fisted the sheets.

"Please."

Prowling between her legs with my staff, I delivered a lick to a nipple. Lust sent me into a spiral at the first touch of her heat. I teased us both mercilessly, rubbing the head of my penis over her sensitive nub repeatedly.

On the next pass, my witch lifted her hips and impaled herself onto me. I let out a hiss and chuckled at her perfect timing. This was going to be fun.

NIKO

I entered the room and bowed to Cyrus's father, Murdox. "You wanted to see me, Sire?"

Murdox glared. "Niko, you have been increasingly negligent when it comes to the updates of my son's life. When is he going to marry Bianca?"

I swallowed back a gag. "Sire, I understand her bloodline is strong, but Bianca would make a horrible queen. She is impossible to predict. Cyrus tires of Bianca and her antics. She is interfering with his personal life. He thinks her a disrespectful nuisance."

Murdox continued to hold me with his eyes. "Cyrus is of my blood. He can control any woman he pleases. Bianca is of no consequence. She will do as she is told. Besides women are to be seen not heard. Unless in the bedroom. Or dungeon." He laughed at his little joke.

I knew all too well Murdox was serious. I stood by countless times as he raped, humiliated, and tortured women. Sometimes boys. Young ones from the training camps, ones without families or homes. He used them and then dispatched them as if they were trash. There had been only one exception. Me.

No, I was the one Murdox made stand guard while he carried out his atrocities. I would have killed him years before had his life not been tied to Cyrus's mother. And by killing the king, I would have forfeited my own life. I couldn't do that to Cyrus or Teagan. Although they are technically my superiors, they are my friends. My brothers.

At first, Murdox used me to spy on his son. As payment of his sins against me I'd planned to kill Cyrus. It wasn't until Cyrus saved my life that I truly noticed the honor and integrity he possessed.

After the training camps, I saw that Cyrus is nothing like his father. Though aggressive, as he would be expected as the king to be, he was also kind, caring, protective, and above all, respectful to everyone. If Cyrus had ever been given special treatment, I hadn't seen it. And that seems to be the way he likes it.

Cyrus does not want to be king. He does not care for riches. He does not care for fame. He cares only for his people, a damn sight more than Murdox has ever shown for those under him. Murdox craves power and will do anything to get it. Entitlement oozes from his pores. It has been said that he had his own father murdered because he coveted his title. There was no doubt in my mind the stories are true.

Murdox interrupted my thoughts. "What personal life does my son have that his future queen cannot be a part of?"

I shrugged. "Sex."

Murdox laughed. "Ha! He can include her. She might like it." He rubbed the outside of his slacks and I felt nausea roll through me. The gesture was the first thing he'd done before assaulting me. He held me down on the floor of a dark pit. The very memory called up the metallic smell of blood and sweat.

I turned to the door, trying to hide my disgust. "Cyrus is expecting me back soon."

CYRUS

A loud voice woke us the next morning.

"Droplet, you want to tell me what the hell is going on here? I don't know if you know this, but there is a naked guy in your bed and a half-million-dollar car in the driveway."

A strange man stood in the door, holding a squirming brown runt.

Gabriela raised up. "God, Hector, stop yelling. What's going on is that you have lost your mind. The guy in the bed is Cyrus. Now get out!"

Hector raised his eyebrows and continued stroking the mutt. "When did you start bringing men home? Were you drunk? Did he drug you? If he did, I'm going to kick his ass."

Gabriela sighed. "Could you chill out for a second?"

"Ho-ly shit!" Hector stared at Gabriela's chest. I hurried to cover her exposing myself in the process. The man's surprise turned to admiration. "Nice." I frowned.

She yelled at Hector to get out, and he turned with a sniff. "Okay…but we *will* be talking about this."

"Yeah. Sure. Whatever. Just get out."

When he was gone, Gabriela fell back onto the bed and covered her face with a pillow. Great infectious peals of laughter came from under it. When we finally caught our breaths, I sent her to the shower and went in search of food.

The kitchen was filled with people. Besides Hector, there was Maddie, Maddie's boyfriend and Avery, a guy I later found out was Hector's boyfriend. At my entrance, silence engulfed the room then a loud guffaw broke all the tension. Questions flew at me. I tried to answer them as best I could.

Then suddenly, the room went quiet. I turned from the stove and locked gazes with my green-eyed goddess. And just like that no one else was in the room. I wondered if she was on the breakfast menu. A hungry look appeared in her eyes as if she read my mind.

"Come to me, Witch," I breathed. Six long strides and a soft brush of her lips had me hard as steel. I pulled back to break the spell. It was either that or take her there on the kitchen floor.

Gabriela glanced over my shoulder and greeted the group. "Good morning."

Hector elbowed Madison. "Good morning to you too. Who's the cutie?"

Madison elbowed him back and smiled at Gabriela. "Don't listen to him. We introduced ourselves to Cyrus before you came down the stairs."

Hector made a noise. "That is *so* not what I meant. What I meant was, who's this cutie to *you*?"

Gabriela looked at me and back at them. "Um…he's… he's my—"

I interrupted her. "…her boyfriend."

The four of them all clapped and she rolled her eyes. "Yeah. Yeah. Yeah. What are you all doing here anyway?"

Mitchell eyed me then answered her. "This was an intervention. You know, because you have been in the house so much."

"We wanted you to know we love you," said Maddie.

"Thanks, you guys. I know you care. I have not doubted that for a second," said Gabriela. "But can you tell me one thing? Whose idea was this?"

Everyone's head turned Madison's way.

Madison held up her arms. "Hey! Don't look at me. It was your mom's."

Gabriela blinked.

Madison grinned. "Well, maybe it was a little me, but how was I to know you were harboring The Hulk in your room? We thought you needed to get out and see the world." She paused for a moment. "We were just worried. Plus, Mitchell needed to ask you something."

Gabriela turned to Mitchell. "What?"

Mitchell blushed. "I wanted to tell you at lunch, but this is as good a time as any. I love Maddie and I want to marry her." Gabriela squealed. Madison held out her hand. A two-carat sparkler sat on her ring finger.

Mitchell continued. "You are like her sister and I didn't want to leave you out of the loop."

Gabriela took Mitchell's hands in hers and stood on tiptoe to kiss his cheek. "There is nothing I love more than to see her happy." She hugged him and then turned to Hector. "You, sir, are in deep crap. What is it with you walking in on me naked?"

She turned to the young man next to him. "I didn't mean to be rude. You must be Avery." Gabriela glanced toward her best friend and grinned. "Hector hit the lotto, didn't he, Maddie?"

"Yes I did," said Hector. "Looks like you did as well." He turned toward me.

"Cyrus, I could look at you all day but I'm sure the men in the room are quite uncomfortable. Could you put something over that work of art you call a chest?" asked Gabriela.

I had forgotten—Gabriela had worn my shirt to the shower. "Sure." I jogged out to my car and grabbed a duffle from the boot. A feeling of unease made the hairs on my neck rise, but after a quick scan around I found nothing out of place. Shaking it off, I went straight to the shower myself. I was fully dressed when the doorbell rang and I heard Gabriela say, "Cyrus's what?!"

Then all hell broke loose.

Bianca licked her lips when she saw me. "Hi, handsome. I was just introducing myself to your new plaything."

Gabriela whipped her head around and glared at me. "Is it true? Are you engaged? And don't insult me by lying."

I knew this was going downhill, but I tried nonetheless. "I would never lie to you. It is not what you think! Ow!"

"GET OUT!"

"Let me explain…" I said, blocking her knee's path to my gonads.

"Get the hell out of my house." The tone of Gabriela's voice shut me up and wiped the smug grin off Bianca's face. I watched in fascination as my witch locked her jaw. Moisture gathered in her beautiful green eyes. She backed me onto the porch and without another word, closed the door. A click announced it was locked.

Silence fell. Bianca and I stood staring at the door. I turned to her, hissing through my teeth. "Bianca Ganas. You have been summoned by the prince and future king of the Phytian tribe." She gasped at my formal words.

"You are summoned to his court and chambers. This is not a request. Your presence is required at 3 p.m. Pray that's enough time for me to regain control or you will need to pick out what shoes you want to wear on your funeral pyre. If you are even one minute late you will not live long enough to regret it. Do you understand?"

She was wide-eyed and pale as a sheet.

"But…"

"YES is the only acceptable answer."

She fell to her knees and I trudged passed her.

Teagan met me at the door of the royal residence. The look on my face must have warned him that his friend was away and the future king was running rampant.

"Request an audience with my father immediately."

"Sire." He acquiesced with a bow.

Thirty minutes later I stood before my mother and father. It was rare they were sighted together during court matters but when it came to issues involving me, my mother did not bend on being in attendance. I kneeled, taking my left fist and beating my chest twice in a warrior's salute to my father. I had changed into my noble's uniform complete with bijou. I never wore the adornment because I seldom had need of it. In the presence of my father, however, not wearing the weapon was a crime as well as a weakness.

"What brings you to me, Son?" Murdox asked, sounding bored. I guess being nearly two hundred years old will do that to a guy.

"I wish to speak freely, Sire."

"Do so."

"I will not mate Bianca."

Niko coughed.

"Why?" asked my father, sitting up straighter.

"I do not love her. You chose her, and with all due respect, you made a horrid decision. Bloodlines be damned. It has taken every discipline you have beaten into me not to permit my second to execute the selfish little ogress. Recently she stepped into affairs which were not her own. I will not take her."

"So be it."

"I ask one more thing of you, Father."

"What?"

"I wish to be given free rein where she is concerned."

"Why? You just refused her all aspects which matter."

"She needs to learn a lesson that I am currently in the right mood to teach."

A hint of a smile appeared on Murdox's puss. "The king within you is showing. Do with her what you will. I am curious, my son. Care to tell me what happened?"

"She approached me about firing my second."

My father stiffened again. "So be it."

"Thank you, Sire."

I left the king's chamber.

"What is your plan?" Teagan asked.

"Homicide." I proceeded to tell him and Niko what happened that morning.

I'd been groomed to rule over others from birth and had failed in my charge. A percentage of the court was mine to control, but since meeting my witch, I had been chucking my duties off onto Teagan. But, after what happened, I knew it would be a long time before I would talk to Gabriela again.

"You shouldn't have had sex with her," Teagan said.

"I know. It was just so damn hard."

"You should've rubbed one out before seeing her. It would've helped."

"Did it help you?" sarcasm dripped from my tone.

He chuckled. "Point taken. Just give her space. In the meantime, busy yourself with work. It is going to take a good week to catch up on your duties."

The throne I sat on was an exact replica of my father's. Oversized iron flames crested the head and armrests. Black leather upholstered the back and seat. Names covered nearly each flame and an indiscernible power oozed from every corner of the structure.

Bianca was prompt. She made no dramatic entrance nor did she pick a fight with Teagan, which was wise. She stopped in her tracks once she saw I was actually sitting on my throne, and remorse rolled across her face. Teagan left her side and sat in a smaller chair to my right. Bianca began to shake. It was not unheard of for a prince to have a co-ruler. But I was the first to invoke the rule in six thousand years. Bianca understood our show of power and fell to her knees.

"Please, Nobles, have mercy on me."

I waved my hand as if swatting a fly. "Cease begging. I will ask you questions and you will answer them. If you lie to me, I will know. Your punishment depends on your answers."

She nodded her head in silence.

"How did you find me at the female's house?"

"I followed you," she muttered.

"Why? And speak up."

"I overheard your plan about getting someone to submit. I became upset."

"You got jealous. You did not just *happen* to overhear an entire conversation," I growled.

"It was not like that. I was trying to save you," she whined.

"Save him from what?" Teagan asked.

"From the mutts! I did not know the female you were sleeping with was human. You kept talking about finding your moiety. No one will take you from me. Had I known what she was, I would not have bothered."

"It is not me you want but the throne. Allow me to inform you on the matter of my queen. You are not and will never be her. I have spoken to my father and it is effective immediately. This will not be your only punishment, however." I looked down at the shriveling heap on the floor below me. "Do you have anything to say in your defense?"

"I was doing it for us. For the tribe. We need pure blood to survive."

"Noted. Anything else?"

Teagan hissed. "Why do you give her such chances? She cannot know the damage she's done. Let me kill her now."

"Easy my brother. Allow her to speak. Bianca?"

"Please do not take my life," she whispered.

"I will not. Instead, I am giving you one. The judgment is as follows: You will be stripped of your title. All bride price accounts will be closed since you are no longer my bride. There will only be an account with what I consider severance pay. You will be given one car, a modest home in town and your bills will be paid two months in advance. You may keep your clothing, shoes, and other personal items. You are no longer welcome to any royal functions or events. Do not communicate with anyone in the court unless they have made an effort to contact you first. No staff will be going with you so make sure you say your goodbyes. Teagan, take Niko and make sure Miss Ganas is packed and completely off the premises by nightfall."

I turned back to Bianca. "Have a wonderful life. You're dismissed."

Niko stepped in to save a passing-out Bianca from smashing her head on the floor.

Teagan gave me a smirk. "Damn, that was good. Wasn't it Niko?"

Niko grinned. It was the least Bianca deserved. She'd come between something I needed and wanted. It wouldn't happen again.

Teagan focused on me with a serious look in his eyes. "Bianca did have a valid point. Gabriela is human. How are you going to approach the subject that you are not only of a different race but the future king?" Only my brothers were witness to Gabby's aura flare. Flares were an anomaly. Usually someone born of either tribe produced a vivid aura. Human's auras were generally bland. Gabriela's had gone from various shades of beige to glittering pastels. This was nothing short of miraculous. Was love enough for her to accept my differences?

I looked back at Teagan. "I don't know brother. I don't know."

GABRIELA

An all too familiar tenor boomed. "What the hell, Gabriela?"

"Hector, how did you get in?"

"With a key. How else? What's wrong with your phone? Your mom called me again." I looked at him in disbelief. He shook his head. "I have no clue why she called me and not Madison."

"Nothing is wrong with my cell."

He grabbed my phone and tapped the screen. "It's dead!"

"See? I told you there was nothing wrong with it."

"Don't play with me, woman. Why did I have to break in here?" I could see he was about to start on a rant sure to burn my ears off.

"The dreams are back."

Hector stopped in mid-sentence. "Damn."

"Yeah. I know. They've been getting stronger and more frequent, even invading my naps. I'm going to handle this on my own, so back off."

"I understand but—"

"No buts. I can do this. Trust me to tell you if I need you."

Sighing deeply, he nodded and wrapped his arms around me. "All right, but if you need anything I am here."

"All right."

"I need you to do something for me before I completely agree or pass on the message to the others."

"What?"

"I need you to get up and clean this house. It's a mess. And while you're at it clean yourself up too. I thought a homeless person had made camp in here."

"Fine. I was thinking about becoming proactive today anyway."

"You really miss him, don't you?" I knew the "he" in question.

I turned on my way to the shower. "Yes, I do."

Hector stayed to watch as I cleaned. I told him about the newest alteration to my dream.

"Wow. I think you should face it head on. I don't mean swimming at the Y either. You have the ocean in your backyard. Just jump in there and get it over with. You can't keep letting this control your life." He thought for a moment. "I'll tell you what. Avery and I are going to Fiji for six months. I will give you that much time to conquer this on your own. But if I come back and you haven't done it, I am telling your mom. Deal?"

"Deal. You're right. This fear is ruining my life."

"I don't care how you do it. I just want you better. Now, I am out of here. It's late and Avery will start to worry. Plus, I need to make sure we've packed everything. Our flight is a week away but I find my love is a procrastinator."

"I can't believe you're leaving me."

"Get over it. Love ya." Blowing a kiss at me, he was gone.

Hector had a point. I had tried everything short of getting into an actual ocean and it all failed. I would jump in tomorrow.

Tomorrow came and went. The entire day, I sat on the pier waiting for the right moment to jump in, but it never came. The next day went the same. By six, I had yet to stick a toe in the water.

"Good idea," I said aloud.

Peeling one leg away from my tightly-coiled body I dangled it over the edge of the pier. My foot hovered inches from the tide. Shutting my eyes tight I moved a little closer. All I had to do was flex my ankle. After taking a deep breath I felt cool wetness wash over my toes. Exhaling, I dipped my other foot in and then slowly leaned back to soak up the last of the sun. I'd made great progress.

Back in the house, I congratulated myself with a huge bowl of strawberry cheesecake ice cream. Hector had seen to it that my phone was fully charged before he'd left, so I checked my messages. There were no texts or calls from Cyrus.

The front door swung open as I rummaged in the fridge for another snack. Madison stood at the entrance to the kitchen. "There is nothing in there. I checked this morning."

"You were here this morning?"

"Yeah. I live here, don't I? You've been so mopey you barely noticed anyone. I am sorry, by the way."

"It's all right. I think he has gotten the message. He hasn't called."

"That's because he's been calling me."

"What?"

"Yeah. I totally don't know how he got my number but yeah. I...uh...I talked to him." She grimaced. "I don't want you to be mad but I think when you are ready you should hear him out. I know it is none of my business but I thought I would just throw that out there. Hey, don't glare at me. I love you and I want you to be happy." She looked over my shoulder into the fridge. "You hungry? I will make something non-vegan–a nice chunk of beef."

I laughed. She was obviously trying to bribe me. "Okay. You just aren't playing fair." I paused. "I want banana pudding too."

"Deal. Now put some clothes on. We need to go to the store."

I marched off. She won this round.

Our shopping cart was nearly overflowing as we approached the produce. "Apples or oranges?" Maddie asked.

"Whatever you want." She had been particularly attentive. Something was going on and I wanted her to spit it out.

"Are you going to do this the entire day? Are you going to tell me?"

"Um…"

"What is it?"

"Mitchell's birthday is tomorrow and I am throwing a party. You've been such a hermit lately. Please say you'll come. You and Hector are my best friends. I would really appreciate it. Please. I'll love you forever."

I sighed and rolled my eyes. "Fine."

She grinned. "You cannot leave until we cut the cake."

"All right."

She gave me the biggest bear hug. Wow. Anyone could see she really loved Mitchell.

The party started out great. Hector, Avery and I met Maddie at Rhett's to set up and decorate. We pulled pranks and told jokes while we worked and at some point, the radio was switched on and a dance party broke out.

Maddie and Hector had Avery and me in stitches with the entire routine of 'N Sync's "It's Gonna Be Me," complete with puppet moves.

All too soon the place was packed with Mitchell's friends and family. The birthday boy practically glowed next to Maddie as he introduced her to everyone. I looked at all the new faces. Two stuck out the most because they seemed to be shooting hostile glances my way. Olivia and Jennifer.

Hector leaned over and whispered in my ear. "You do something to those bitches?"

"Hmmm. So, I am not seeing things. They really *are* looking at me like that."

"Oh, yeah. Want me to ask them what the fuck?"

"No. I'm sure it is nothing."

"Okay, but I've got your back."

I winked at him. "I know. I'm going to grab another plate. Want something?"

Hector shook his head.

The kitchen door slammed hard behind me and I spun around. Olivia stood, blocking the door. Her face was blotchy.

"Hello, Olivia."

"I know you are seeing Rhett behind my back. Jennifer told me."

I blinked. "Okay," I said stretching out the syllables. "There's a misunderstanding here. I was and am not seeing Rhett. He was just my escort for one night. We have never gone on a date nor even talked about it. I am not interested in him at all." She frowned. I walked around her.

Everyone sat eating and conversing in the living room. Maddie had cooked vegan lasagna, Mitchell's favorite dish, and was giving him what had to be his fourth helping. He stared at her with so much affection and heat that I nearly blushed.

The look made me think of another pair of eyes and I knew I needed some air. Thinking of Cyrus was a sure way to cause my body to overheat. Ten minutes passed before I could get alone. Rhett's place was on the water's edge, as were many of the homes on the island. Wandering toward the beach, I slipped my sandals off and enjoyed the night air.

My toes sifted through the sand. Soft waves crept to meet me and I felt the shifting grains under my feet. I took a couple more steps until the water reached my ankles. It felt nice.

A small shimmering object partially buried in the sand was revealed by the moonlight. I bent to pick it up. It was a metal shell.

"What's that?" said Rhett. I'd had no idea that he'd followed me out.

"I just found it."

He grinned. "Well, finders keepers."

"Thanks." I placed the tiny shell in my pocket.

Rhett cleared his throat. "Look, I felt like an idiot about what happened. I never got a chance to break up with her in person. I told her it was over that night at the club." His face radiated sincerity.

"I don't understand." That only seemed to agitate him.

"You know, when you caught Olivia kissing me. I know you were hoping you and I could make something happen. I didn't know she was going to be there."

"Okay. Wait a minute. You are apologizing to me for kissing your girlfriend?"

"Yeah."

"Because you thought I wanted you?"

"Yeah. I figure you owe me an apology too. For the way you were grinding all over that guy when I left. You looked like a tramp."

I stepped back. Whoa. He needed a jacket, like the strait kind. The last thing I needed to get into was someone else's romantic problems. I was having my own. I turned on my heels and started toward the house. I passed Olivia on the way.

Once inside, Maddie and I locked eyes. "I love you. See you later." I mouthed.

She nodded and mouthed it back but a ghost of a frown crossed her face. I caught Hector's eye and signaled for him to call me later. He nodded and smiled.

By the time I got home, I was still fuming. Owe Rhett an apology? What a joke. I slid on a silk nightgown and climbed into bed. I just wanted the day over.

The strumming of a guitar startled me into wakefulness and I sat up, blinking my eyes. Sunbeams streamed into the room. "Hello?" I said through a fog.

"Gabriela, it's Hector." His voice broke. "It's Madison. There was a fire. She… She is in the hospital."

I sat up straight in bed. "What? Which hospital?"

"East Brunswick."

I was on my feet in a flash. "I'm leaving now."

Throwing on the clothes I had worn the night before, I was out the door in seconds.

My heart hammered in my chest. Tears flowed unchecked until I arrived at the hospital. Hector stood outside, waiting for me.

"Droplet!" he shouted. His arms crushed me to him. "It's... It happened so fast. I was leaving and that's when I saw the flames. I didn't know what to do." His hand shook as he held an unlit cigarette to his lips.

"Where is she?"

"Room 420. I'll show you."

Mitchell sat in an armchair by Maddie's side. She simply looked asleep, except for the oxygen mask. Smudges of soot dotted her skin, but there were no obvious burns.

I frowned and looked at Hector. "Mitchell knows everything," he said.

Mitchell blinked bloodshot eyes as if I'd appeared by magic. His face and clothes were covered in ash. Tears tracked down his cheeks. His mouth opened and then shut before he broke into a soul-wrenching sob.

"I tried to save her but she fainted in my arms. The doctor said it's severe smoke inhalation. She has awful burns in her lungs and trachea. They don't think she's going to make it through the night. Her parents are on the way"

His voice cracked. A sharp pain twisted viciously in my stomach, and I felt myself crumple to the cold tile floor. I heard Mitchell again, as if in an echo chamber. "I tried to save her. I tried to breathe for her until the ambulance came."

Sound faded under the rhythm of my racing heart and my own lungs burned as everything blurred. If only I had stayed.

My name was the last thing I heard before darkness engulfed me.

"Teagan, I'm done. You handle anything else. Bunch of whiny sissies." I made a face and mocked the woman who had just rushed away. "'The training camp is too hard on my grandson. He comes home all black and blue.' What the hell did the biddy think they did in a training camp? Knit?"

"Good thing we are done for the day, isn't it?" said my smartass lieutenant.

"You watch it bro."

Teagan waved his hand at me. "Do not start your bitching with me. I understand why you are so wired. I am bonded, so I get women issues too. Sometimes I swear they were put on this planet to make it hard for men. But I'm gonna kick your ass if you keep this up. You are in one hell of a mood."

"Am not. I am just done with the whining."

"Dude, you made someone's grandma cry."

"Shut up."

Pouting a little myself, I knew he was right. It had been two weeks since I'd found out about Madison's death. Teagan and I had gone and watched the funeral from afar. He'd counseled me, saying that Gabriela did not need to deal with our issues while burying someone she loved.

I figured she would reach out for me in time, but she hadn't. I needed to hold and comfort her. Every instinct in me rebelled against giving her more time. After a week of calling, I had given up and gone to her house. No one was there. Nor had they been there on any day since.

Nothing had ever made me lose my cool but this thing with Gabriela was cracking me wide open. I missed spending time with her the most. If only she wasn't human—she would not be able to stay away from her mate for so long. The stress of it would have driven her crazy.

I found myself hating her genetics more than anything. Without a doubt, I knew she was my moiety. The connection was there and her aura had changed. On the other hand, Gabriela did not seem to feel the effects as I did. I kept tabs on her through Madison but now with her gone, I had no connection with Gabriela.

Other questions arose once I had taken everything into account. First, was it possible to produce offspring with a human? Our race didn't have many differences. Simply put, we had an extra chromosome. According to our medics, the anomaly gave us the ability to use a greater percentage of our brains than humans, and even more with a bijou. In the histories of the Phytians or Allus, nothing about mating with humans had ever been recorded. We could have sex with them but no children ever were produced.

On the other hand, Madison once shared that Gabriela was crying in her room a lot.

"It is like she is grieving. I don't understand. You guys hadn't known each other long. She has never acted this way before," Madison said. I kept busy, but she hadn't. It only made sense. No one around her would understand the emptiness one felt without her mate.

It would only get worse when the ritual was done. How she would deal with my being a part of another race was something entirely up in the air. The fact that one day I would be king of the Phytians was a topic I felt I should broach gently.

Niko spoke with such urgency that it snapped me out of my musings. "Sire!"

I rolled my eyes. "Yes?"

"There is something you need to see."

I tried to brush past him. "All court engagements go to Teagan."

"Sire," he whispered, refusing to move.

I glared at him. "Do you want me to kill you, my brother?"

"You would kill me if I did not tell you what I have found. It is about Madison Hart."

Teagan stood to the side.

I stilled. "Natural?"

Niko swallowed hard. "Um…"

"Natural or summoned?" I demanded.

"Both."

"Show us," growled Teagan.

We were whisked away and found ourselves standing in front of the ruined beach house where Madison spent her last hours. I pulled my bijou from my pocket and put it on. The adornment was similar to that of my mother's, a thin yellow-gold torc with a black stone on the tip. It was small and flimsy for someone my size but it served its purpose well.

Walking over to a part of the home's framework that the fire managed only to singe, I touched it and opened my senses. I knew instantly.

"Do you know whose flame this is?" I demanded.

Niko shook his head. "No."

The fire had been born of the Phytian. It started naturally but had been imbedded. Tiny threads of a signature were definitely present. They were unique to the owner, like fingerprints. One thing tied one to another; a thin filament attached a person to a particular bloodline.

As prince, I am aware of most summoned flames and those I do not know, my second usually does. I looked to Teagan. He also shook his head. "It is no one we have met before."

Teagan paused. "Look, I need a fucking drink and to see my Phoebe. Tonight, we will hit Sclavus and brainstorm."

"Yes," I growled. Killing humans was against tribal laws. Whoever had done this would pay.

Sorin became aware of two things upon waking. One, a woman was in his lair. Two, she was lying on his back.

Of course, he knew who she was. Last week, he'd been awakened when the crazed harpy dropped a rather large stone on his head. He'd thought at first it was assassins and had prepared to kill anyone in the area but after removing the hunk of burning granite from his skull he considered stealth as his better option.

In human form, he'd gone topside via a back way and concealed himself in the trees. A short raven-haired banshee stood in the middle of the clearing throwing blazing boulders into the opening of his cave. Her skin was the color of sun-sanded beaches and her eyes the richest ebony.

As Sorin watched, he became fascinated with the amount of focus and discipline she used to lift objects double her weight. Sweat covered her face and determination furrowed her brow. He found her intriguing and unbelievably sexy. He watched her every day this week from afar before realizing she was his mate. He'd still

129

been deciding whether to approach her before taking his nap. Now here she was dismounting him.

Sorin remained still, not wanting to scare the little imp. He waited and thought she would be across the cavern when he opened his eyes. The contact was instant and he knew it was too late for them both. She woke from her fainting spell and commenced wailing again.

He projected his voice. "I will not hurt you, Little One."

Immediately she stopped screaming. Her eyes narrowed. She took in short startled puffs and then suddenly squared her shoulders.

"Do not call me that. And... And I know what you are. So... So you just come on out of there." She meant business.

Sorin grinned inside the demon. If she wanted him out... He would come out.

***

Amaryl watched in amazement as her piece of sculpted furniture morphed into Michelangelo's David. Her brain seized as she got an eyeful of his delicious body. Lust burst forth with enough power that she took an involuntary step forward. *I am going to lick every inch of that skin,* she thought.

"For goodness sakes you're naked!" she croaked.

"Did you think the Banumi wore clothing in their demon form, Little One?"

She stared at his backside, thinking that it would give any of Calvin's models glute envy. "Why did you let me ramble on like that?"

"You wanted to talk and I wanted to listen." He shrugged and walked away. "Why were you about to kiss me?"

"To thank what I thought was a sculpture for listening to my ranting."

She continued to eye hump him. *I don't know this man. He's certainly not my mate.*

"Are you sure?"

"Sure of what?"

131

"Are you sure I am not your mate? And, by the way, my name is Sorin, not Calvin." She froze, thoughts racing through her head. *I did not say that out loud!*

"No. You did not."

The implications hit her. It was rumored Banumi only had telepathy with their mates. She'd done it. She'd found her mate. He was a demon. She didn't care.

"Would you submit to a monster? A beast?" he turned to look at her. His eyes showed genuine curiosity as he pulled on a pair of pants from... well, she didn't know where. Her eyes lowered to his hips and fixed. He was fully erect. "Little One?"

"Hmm?"

"Submission?" She nodded furiously. It seemed she lost the ability to speak full sentences.

Sorin chuckled again. "Want to do it now?"

Her eyebrow crinkled. "Tomorrow?" She had to get a few things in order first.

He gazed at her. *"Your aura has changed already. How will you explain it? I am Banumi and can't be seen, but it will put you in too much danger."* He paused for a moment, reflecting. *"Are you sure you want to do this? I should court you properly or at the very least know your name."*

"My name is Amaryl Kier. I am Phytian-born and betrothed to Murdox Zorn, but once I am claimed by you, he will have to go away. It is law. There is no need for courtship. I will protect you and your secret. You are good. I have a sense of these things. We will do the claiming tomorrow."

"Are you so eager to be out of this Murdox's grasp that you would give yourself to a monster?"

She shook her head. *"No, not a monster. I'm submitting to my real mate. Now, there will be no more talk of him. I have to get ready for tomorrow."* She looked around. *"Is there another way out of here? I floated down earlier."*

Sorin shook his head in amazement. He could see the truth in the words she spoke. She was actually going to permit his claim of her.

***

Try as he might, Sorin could not shake the excitement of seeing his little harpy again. The past week had been the best of his existence. Somehow he'd managed to talk Amaryl into postponing the claiming ritual and was courting her as properly as he could.

They would go into towns far away from her home to avoid Phytians. He knew that the closer they were, the more dangerous it was for her to be seen with him.

Amaryl learned that Sorin was a great dancer. Visiting nightclubs and seducing him with her moves was one of her favorite things to do. Each movement mimicked the act of lovemaking.

Sorin was finding it harder to say no to her advances with every passing day. He wanted to wait for a month, according to ritual, but the longer he was in her presence the more he thought it an impossibility.

The need to claim one's mate could cause difficulties at best. He was beginning to understand what that really meant. Every time Amaryl looked at him—which was often—he would harden. It had quickly become apparent how futile it would be to keep her from noticing his erections. She would stare at his hips for long periods of time then send him detailed fantasies with her thoughts. It was the sweetest torture. Today would be different, however. He'd taken care to wear loose fitting pants.

***

Amaryl made her way to the cave. Enough was enough. Sorin would claim her today. She was done with being courted. Tonight.

She'd taken special precautions this time. She'd done some research on the claiming ritual. Her family's library was extensive and every morning her parents were away, she spent time looking for the proper ammunition for her mission. She'd found the answer on the previous morning and had perfected it today. Yesterday she had been able to close part of her mind to Sorin. Extreme measures had to be taken—seducing him like a normal man was not working.

Entering the cave, she took in the sight of his golden eyes, broad shoulders, and tapered waist. Then she gawked at him. He was clothed in Pelle jeans. "What are you wearing?!"

"They're more comfortable."

"For your boner?"

"Yes." He laughed.

"Then you'll be pleased to know that we are staying in. I baked you cookies. Here," She crooned with just the right amount of innocence. "Could you put a fire there? I am a little chilly."

An opening appeared in the earth exactly where she pointed. A few moments later glowing red stones filled the pit and a lovely smell of spices permeated the air. The cavern lacked modern conveniences like indoor plumbing or electricity but there was a small water feature to one side of the cave.

Earlier in the week she managed to talk Sorin into getting a bed. He did not care for one, he had said, but he would always put her needs above his own. Amaryl sat on the bed and watched as Sorin popped the last of the sweet treats into his mouth.

"Like them, did you?"

"Very much. Before you bashed my brains in with that stone I estivated for many years. So this is truly a gift," *he admitted.*

She laughed. "Really? It is a good thing that tiny pebble landed where it did, now isn't it?"

"Pebble?" he asked, grinning. "If I wasn't immune to death, I would have been crushed."

His gaze softened. "I will not be immune after the ritual," he admitted.

She returned his gaze. "Are you upset about that?"

"No, not at all."

She searched his face. "Good. Because I want to be claimed tonight."

"Little One, we have already discussed this. Remember? You said I could have one more month of courting without your seducing me."

"I don't have to seduce you. You are going to do that all on your own."

***

Sorin's eyes narrowed at Amaryl's words. Before he could ask her what she meant an explicit scene appeared vivid in his cortex.

Shaking his head, Sorin sat next to her and felt his engorged member twitch. What was wrong with him? Amaryl tilted her head toward his. Her beautiful black hair formed a curtain as she gave him the softest of kisses.

When she pulled away he noticed there was something different about her. Something more... more mischievous? She was every bit the harpy he'd named her, enticing, angelic, and wicked all at the same time.

The temptress rose from the bed to kneel at his feet. Everything inside Sorin stilled and his body went rigid. Inside him, a beast of a new kind stirred. Amaryl looked into his eyes, licked her lips, and lowered her head in submission. She would become moiety to this male tonight.

She had one last thing to do before lowering her shield.

Going back in her mind over the past week, she mentally told him how she felt about their time together. Memories of their talks and dancing; memories of their kisses and how his touch made her feel. She heard an erotic rumble and knew she was on the right track.

She pulled up her fantasies next, strategically placing them in order. The first one caused her to be yanked off her knees to stand chest to chest with Sorin. She squared her shoulders and took a step back to peer into his eyes. What she saw there took her breath. His irises were no longer gold, but the darkest of blacks. She took another step back and fed him the next fantasy.

"Stop," he commanded in a growling tone. She took another step and he watched her every move.

Amaryl had heard the legend that the Banumi had animalistic traits and she knew she was dealing with a predator. Males of her kind were their most savage before the claiming. If the tales of Sorin's race were true, he would be uncontrollable. His instinct would be the only thing driving him and her complete submission would be the only solution. Amaryl was so aroused she could smell her own scent calling to Sorin.

When his self-control broke, she would make a run for it. She pushed forward her most detailed fantasy and saw the moment he reached some sort of peak.

By this time, she had successfully put the length of the cave between them. Now to push him over the cliff.

Staring into his now black eyes, she put the final phase of her plan in action by opening her mind completely. and then ran for all she was worth. She had barely made it through to the woodlands when a piercing roar reached her ears.

He was on her in a matter of seconds, pinning her to a tree and stripping her of her bottoms. He was not gentle or tame in his claiming. Nor was he overly forceful. It was perfect. They made love there in the open with the stars and moon above them.

Awareness returned to Amaryl a piece at a time. Despite the fact that her body felt like it had been hit by an eighteen-wheeler, the night before had surpassed everything she had ever hoped for. After the first time, Sorin made gentle love to her for most of the night. He had been angry at her ambush but understood her reasons once they were fully connected. The claiming itself was excruciatingly painful for them both. She now understood why nature had the female submit. No one would go through such agony for an unworthy mate. And hers was more worthy than most. They now shared memories as well as heartbeats.

Waking to a sleeping Sorin made her heart swell with pride. He was hers. She had found her true mate and could hardly wait to tell her parents.

She decided not to wake him until she'd told her family about the claiming. She wrote a note explaining her absence if he awoke before she returned. She expected her family to be concerned—they had already noticed a change in her aura.

Excitement and joy coursed throughout her body as she left the cave and ran through the woodlands. There would be no marriage to Murdox Zorn!

She passed the worship center, jogged through the market and turned toward the library. She had been running so fast she was unable to stop when suddenly, an obstacle appeared—Cain, second to Murdox.

A brute in his own right, Cain was more of his leader's lapdog than what his position called for. He held up his hand, bringing her to a halt.

He stared at her with an odd expression. "Where are you going in such a hurry?"

Amaryl tried to maneuver out of his way. "Home. Excuse me."

"Where have you been?" he demanded.

"None of your business. Now if you don't mind I have to go."

"I'll rephrase that. Where the fuck have you been?"

"I believe I told you it was none of your business."

"I was sent to retrieve you. You are to be Murdox's mate. Your parents are aware of this and have given their blessing."

"You mean you bullied them into compliance! You are wrong. I will not be with Murdox. I am already bonded."

"Your aura shows you are lying. You have bonded with no one. Perhaps your mate has found you, yes. But he does not own you. You are Zorn's property."

"Owned? Property?" she huffed. "I assure you I am bonded. It is very new, but my aura will change. And by no means am I owned or property of anyone. It would be a cold day in hell before I would willingly submit to Murdox."

A sneer appeared on Cain's face. "Such disrespect. The hard way it is."

One minute she was standing toe to toe with Cain. The next a sweet-smelling cloth was forcefully placed over her mouth and nose. Red spots appeared over her vision a moment before the world went dark.

GABRIELA

Two weeks passed since Maddie's death. I couldn't stand to be in the house, so Oscar and I moved from the island to the house in the gated community in Phoenix.

I hated it. It was hot and lonely, but Mom, Trent, and Hector refused to leave my side and I needed time alone.

Mom insisted that I come home with her, but Hector reassured her he would keep an eye on me. It took a week before she would set foot in an airport. They didn't need to see my sorrow.

Sleep was virtually non-existent. My night terrors worsened, but it was no longer me who was drowning. It was Madison.

To occupy my mind, I joined the local gym and volunteered at a suicide call center. Providing support to others made me remember there were bigger issues than my own.

Even so, my life was in complete disarray. Moving to Phoenix and getting a new cell phone number had not changed my feelings about Cyrus. I missed him like crazy and compared him to every cute guy I met. No matter how hot the guy, Cyrus's golden gaze always broke any tie.

The ringing phone shook me from my musings. "Ms. Blair?"

"Yes?"

"This is Detective Victor Moore. I am calling because we were notified of a break-in at your house on Crest Wolf Lane. Is there a way you could come in and give us your statement?"

"A break in? Uh... Yes, but I am not in the city now. I can be there tomorrow."

After exchanging information with Detective Moore, I booked a flight and arranged for Oscar to stay in a nice pet hotel. Then I called the only friends I could count on. Hector and Avery volunteered to pick me up from the airport and insisted I stay with them.

145

Their place was suave with minimalist taste. It had a monochromatic theme but still gave a cozy vibe. I changed into my warmest pajamas and flopped onto the bed.

"Comfy? We just thought we would check on you before hitting the sack." Avery said.

"I know it is late, but thank you both. I know you postponed your trip because of everything that happened. I am glad you are finally leaving tomorrow. You deserve some happiness."

"So do you," said Hector. "Now get some shut eye."

The next day was a blur. The police interview and walk-through showed nothing was missing, but my home was definitely ransacked—a few chairs were turned over, papers were tossed across the room and the back door kicked in. Nothing else was broken. Later, Hector and I had lunch with Mitchell—he appeared to be doing about the same as me—just making it.

A phone call from Detective Moore heralded a surprise. When he asked me on a date, no one was more shocked than me. But when Victor mentioned the reopening of Club Sclavus, it gave me pause.

I suggested dinner only but he insisted on dancing. I was still hesitant. What were the chances Cyrus would be there on a Thursday? After all, every time we ran into each other, it had been on the weekend.

I agreed to meet him and showed up a bit early. The rebuilt Sclavus resembled the original, lasers and spray tans. A larger dance floor and better air flow were the only noticeable differences. My attention was gripped when the melodic notes of Florence Welsh danced around the building. I clinched my fist trying to stop the flood of memory. Snatching my purse from the table I stumbled from the establishment. I would text Victor when I reached the car. What had I been thinking?

"Excuse me, Miss. You left ya phone." I turned and came face to face with a large man.

"Oh, thank you." I reached for it, but the man grabbed my wrist.

"Let go of me!" I yelled, looking around for some kind of weapon. Taking a deep breath to calm my nerves, I tried to gather my wits. I'd watched a show on Spike once about "Easy Ways to Defend Yourself." What did the guy say? *Talk calmly.* Yeah, that is a good start. "Umm…Sir. Would you mind letting go of me?"

"Where ya going? I was about to ask ya to dance when ya left without yo phone. I thought to myself, 'Self, that is a sign if I'd ever saw one.' I caught you just in the nick of time. This was fate and I'm not going to let ya go 'til ya dance with me." He reeked of alcohol and B.O.

"I am not a good dancer." I pretended to think. "I'll tell you what, program your number into my cell. You can sober up and teach me how to dance all day tomorrow."

"Or he can take his damn hands off of you and live to *see tomorrow*," snarled from the darkness. My "dance partner" paled and released his hold immediately. He began to back away slowly with his palms raised.

"I didn't know she was yours. Really," stammered Nathan. He turned and ran at top speed back to the club. I decided not to tempt fate and dashed toward my car,

148

when the voice spoke again. "Leaving me without saying a word again, Love? It has been weeks. I miss you." The disembodied voice echoed in the emptiness. I moved faster. "Frightened? Oh, my beautiful witch, you should be. I am coming for you tonight. You will not keep hiding from me. Not from me."

I was flat out sprinting now. Sprinting away from the power I could feel racing toward me. Pulling my keys from my purse, I could almost smell the feral scent and bergamot of my predator. Once inside the car, I started it with a roar and peeled the hell out of there. I chided myself. *What were you thinking? He knows you are back now.*

I had to get my things first. I hadn't had time to unpack. I just needed to throw my bath products into a bag. I could be in and out in a flash. Parking in the front, I took out everything that belonged to me. A valet agreed to return the rental car and hail me a cab. I was back down with all my things in less than five minutes. The valet had a town car waiting. I watched as my things were placed into the trunk, and sighed in relief as the driver opened the door.

I slumped in the seat and closed my eyes, savoring the fact that I would be long gone before morning's first light.

"Ma'am?" the driver asked as the doors locked.

"Yes?" I breathed.

"Sire sends his regards for not coming himself." He looked at me in the rearview and smiled. "I was told to follow his instructions carefully and tell you that you can only exit this vehicle if someone with a key opens it from the outside. I do not have this key. Once the door is closed, I cannot exit either."

His words sent a chill down my spine. Now I was trapped and the bastard made sure there was no way to escape. Even if I could talk the driver into letting me go, how would he get out? Locking the driver in. Who has ever heard of such a thing?

After a 20-minute ride, I began to feel like the Fresh Prince himself. Newly clipped grass and hedges spread out across acres of land. A massive white estate house loomed proudly at the peak of a hill. Suddenly, I remembered I'd never asked Cyrus what he did for a living. Whatever it was it must be major league.

My heart started to beat wildly as both the driver and I sat in the car waiting for someone to release us from our motorized cell. Minutes passed like hours. Hours like days. I was about to open my mouth when the front door of the mansion opened and a stacked young woman with ebony skin stepped out.

Rachel. Too busy rearranging her clothes to notice my glare, she walked right by me as I sat in the 4-wheeled prison. I slumped further into my seat turning to stretch my legs out. Glaring at the back of the driver's head, I kicked off my stiletto. Suddenly the partition went up and I caught his smug smile in the rearview a moment before it closed. Mentally exhausted and pissed off I snuggled as close as I could to the back of the car's seat.

***

I felt arms wrap around me and burrowed closer to them as they rocked me. The scent of earthy wildness and bergamot would make a woman who had just eaten a six-course meal salivate. I inhaled deeper. I wanted to roll around in it. To bathe in it. "Missed me, did you?"

My eyes snapped open. Cyrus.

He grinned. "I was wondering when I would get the chance to hold you again."

"You bastard!" I yelled. When he dropped me onto a firm bed, I tried to slam my fist into his stupid handsome face. "You bastard!"

"You're repeating yourself, Love," he said calmly. I fixated on the exit. Sensing that pushing was not the best thing, I tried sweet talk. Perhaps I could get out of here if I was nicer, but he was throwing off all kinds of sexual heat. I had to tread lightly.

"Umm," I said in my most sugary voice while sliding toward the opposite side of the bed. "Hi. Nice to see you again. How…ah…ya been?" I asked, glancing toward the door.

Cyrus trapped my ankle with his hand. "Try it. I dare you. You just try to run away from me again."

I shook my head keeping my eyes downcast.

"Look at me!"

I shook my head again.

He gripped my chin with his thumb and forefinger and I was forced to comply. "You shouldn't have left me," he said. "I am so sorry about Maddie. I understood you leaving that house but I wanted to console you in your need." He ran a hand through his hair and began to pace. "I am going to talk. Will you listen?"

I nodded.

"Yes, I was *betrothed* but not engaged. Meaning I did not pick her as my mate. It is not the same. Yes, I should have told you. I'm sorry for that. I did not mean to hurt you. It is so rare to find one's moiety." Pain was clearly etched on his face. "My father chose her."

"Stop. Find a what? No, don't tell me. I don't care. Betrothed, engaged, married, is all the same to me. You touched me knowing you belonged to another woman. Have you any idea how sleazy I felt? No, you don't. Then, you kidnap me like we are in a SAW movie! Have you lost your mind? Never mind the fact that I just watched that chick from the restaurant catwalk out of this very house while you left me to rot in the backseat of a town car!"

We were chest to chest as I stood on my tiptoes. Panting, I said, "I want nothing from you. I have a plane to catch. You stay away from me, Married Man, and I won't gut you. Deal?"

His face went completely expressionless. "You will rest here tonight. When you wake, a different car will take you where you need to go. I will do as you ask and leave you alone, for now. But think about what I said." He paused. "I missed you." The door clicked softly behind him. I breathed a sigh of relief.

After a moment of calm I began to notice the splendor around me. The accommodations were spectacular. There were heated marble floors, crown moldings and a jetted tub surrounded by silk draperies the color of Cyrus's eyes. The tub was too inviting to turn down. After rummaging around in a few drawers, I found a black satin robe, an unopened toothbrush and a bottle of lavender lotion.

It did not take long to fill up the large whirlpool. I'd stripped off the navy slip dress I wore for my date with Victor when a glint off a shiny white box in the corner caught my eye, a stereo. The soft sounds of modern jazz seeped into the space. I swayed to the music while divesting the rest of my clothing.

The water felt like soft caresses on my sensitive flesh. *If this is what being a kidnapped victim feels like I am getting snatched every weekend.*

The next day I found Cyrus to be a man of his word. I was given everything he'd promised. Almost. "That should do it, Miss," said a sweet young man.

I smiled and nodded. "Thank you."

He smiled back. "The security guy just left. Do you remember the code?"

"Yes."

"All right. Call us if you need anything else."

 "She will," said my new guard dog. The driver, who had finally told me his name was Teagan, was now standing in my house overseeing all repairs. Somehow, he'd managed to make me miss the plane. After that, I had been given two choices. Go back to Cyrus's estate or go home. When I picked the latter, he did not appear shocked but his mood had definitely darkened. It had gone from dark to pitch black when I told him about the break-in.

After that, he was on his cell for 20 minutes talking to someone I was 99.9 percent sure was Cyrus. He tried talking me into coming back for another forty minutes. Eventually, we compromised. I could stay at home if the door were fixed. Teagan stood by while a security company wired the place tighter than Fort Knox. Once the two companies showed, Teagan received another call from the wife, I guessed. There were a bunch of "Honeys" and "I won'ts" and a couple of "I will pick it up next times." It ended with an "I love you."

I smiled. What I'd thought was a German Shepherd was actually a Yorkshire. It was kind of funny, but endearing to see a man the size of a large SUV crouched over a phone trying to appease what was no doubt the love of his life.

He turned to me the color of tomato sauce. "You are settled, so I will be going. But if you need anything call me. I mean it. You might not want anything to do with Cyrus but my loyalty lies with him and by extension, you. I will do whatever needed to keep you safe." He left without another word. The man was so loyal it made me think again to ask Cyrus what he did for a living.

By nightfall, the house looked normal again. Tiredness set in and I all but fell onto the sofa. Flipping on the television, I was out before one word was spoken.

A moon sat full behind a cache of massive soot colored rain clouds. Enormous waves crashed to shore. Cool night air swirled hair around my face and the scent of rain was heavy. Thunder rolled somewhere in the distance. The hem of my black satin robe was burned and

ragged. Tears trickled down my chin as the moon broke
through the clouds and spilt its light upon my skin.
Slowly I walked into the embrace of the sea. Its surf
engulfed me. Walking as deep as my lungs would take me
I closed my eyes, submerged my head, and inhaled. There
was no intense panic. No screaming or burning lungs.
Only peace and tranquility filled me. It was my choice. I
was absolute in my willingness.

I sat up, gasping for air. W-T-F? Suicide? I moved to get up and fell right off the sofa. It was not looking to be a good day. Then my cell buzzed. I knew who it was without bothering to look.

"Cyrus, I just woke up. Leave me alone until I have had breakfast at least."

"Uh…okay. I hate it for Cyrus."

"Hector? What time is it?" I asked, still groggy.

"Two p.m. tomorrow."

I blinked. Understanding dawned and I burst out laughing. "I'm glad to hear that again," he admitted.

"What?"

"Your laughter. It has been so long. I just wanted to let you know we made it to Fiji okay. It is gorgeous. I don't think we are ever leaving. You should join us when you get everything settled."

"I might just do that."

While I was explaining to Hector about my busted date and missing my flight, my cell beeped.

"That must be Cyrus now. Call me when you can. Love you."

"Love ya too." I clicked over. "Cyrus?"

"No...this is your mother."

Questions rushed at me from all angles. "Why haven't you called since you have gotten to the island? Hector told Trent it had been broken into. Are you all right?" It took two hours before she was calm. It took another twenty-five minutes to get her off the phone.

Cyrus didn't call that day or the next. I tried to schedule a Sunday flight back to Phoenix but all were booked. The next available flight wasn't until Wednesday, so I was stuck in the house with no car, no Hector, and worst of all, no Maddie.

Another day passed without a call from Cyrus and my panic began to grow. "God, what is wrong with me?" I asked no one. I pushed shaky hands through my hair. I was mad at him but not to the point that I wanted him to vanish. The lack of communication between us was making me mental. My mind kept telling me something horrible had happened to him. I had tried, unsuccessfully, to will my cell to ring for the past 24 hours.

"Enough!" I snatched it up and dialed.

"I am here, Love. I'm fine," he said quickly. I exhaled the breath I did not know I was holding. Finding a seat, I plopped down in relief. My entire body was still shaking.

"I know. I am here," he whispered.

"How did you know?"

"Because you are my moiety," he said as if it were simple.

"Okay, pretend like I don't know what that word means. In English, this time. Please."

"Can I see you? We need to talk." He was changing the subject.

"I don't know. I am still mad at you."

"Just think about it."

"We will talk but not now. Now that I know you are not dead, I can get some sleep."

"I understand. Have sweet dreams."

I hung up. I didn't really need to sleep but what I wanted to do was personal.

It only took a moment to put on my swimsuit. Today was the day I was going to jump off that damned dock into the sea. Ever since my nightmare took on a suicidal twist, I had become more determined to face it.

Grabbing a towel, I all but marched to the edge of the pier. Dropping the fabric on the deck I took several steps back and inhaled. Nervousness shot up my spine but I began to run. All too soon I was out of runway. My body plummeted into the ocean's cool depths. I surfaced to release a breath. Briny liquid dripped into my eyes when I raised my lids.

Pure joy surged through me when I saw that I had done it. A squeal of excitement came from me, and I began to laugh out loud. Short waves splashed all around, only causing me to laugh harder. I absorbed the feeling of triumph. Nothing had ever felt so right. My dad and Maddie would have been proud.

A flash of red to the right of me caught my attention, but it disappeared before I could figure out what it was. Then something brushed against my left side. I looked down into the surf but still didn't see anything.

"It is about damn time." An unknown baritone boomed. "I have been looking for you for ages." Startled, I turned to see a red-headed beast of a man floating beside me.

"I'm sorry. What?"

The man rolled his eyes. He lifted his hand to his lips and put what looked like a rock in his mouth. "Looking. For. You," the giant repeated while using American Sign Language.

I blinked. He rolled his eyes. "You *look* like her but you most definitely aren't her. I gather you are a bit daft."

"Who are you?" I asked incredulously.

"My name is Sebastian. Now, let's get going." He wrapped a strong arm around my waist and dove deep. Caught off guard, my fight or flight response came fast. I kicked, scratched and screamed. I watched as an enormous hole open before us right there in the middle of the ocean! The idiot was swimming right for it and I wailed in warning.

Sebastian tightened his arm around my waist. "Calm down, will ya? We are almost there." Once we reached the mouth of the vortex, I shut my eyes and dug my nails into Sebastian's wrist.

"Dammit, woman. If you aren't careful your nails are gonna slice open my radial artery."

He set me down on my feet, I wiggled my toes and felt sand. Opening one eye to survey our new surroundings, I realized it was dark. Just a moment before the sun had been bright and high in the sky.

I took a step back and turned in a circle. There was no way we were on the island. I wasn't even sure we were still on Earth.

A tug on my arm brought me back to the present and to the brute who had so callously tried to drown me. He was flat on his back and I was sitting on his chest in an instant.

Sebastian gasped. "Maybe you *are* like her."

My hands were wrapped around his thick throat and I was debating on squeezing but I needed answers first. "What the hell are you talking about? Why did you try to kill me? You had better start talking or you're about to run out of oxygen."

He grunted. "I'll adapt." I felt his neck flex. There was a light fluttering on both of my palms and I loosened my grip then screamed.

"Usually when a woman screams while sitting on top of me I am flattered," the ass said with a smirk. I slapped him, and his smirk widened to a grin. He slapped me back.

"I'm a girl. You aren't supposed to hit a girl!" I exclaimed and attacked.

Another male voice boomed. "Sebastian! You couldn't wait to get her up to your room? Did you have to have her out here? I have seen you do some strange things but this by far is the most insane. What if Osun sees?"

Sebastian shook his head. "This daft girl obviously isn't one of mine."

I slapped him again.

"Don't just stand there, Shade. Get her off of me!"

"That better be the last time you call me that or someone better have mercy on you because I won't." I threatened.

The new man's mouth dropped. "She slapped you!?"

Finally lifting my head, I glared at the newest buffoon. He had an athletic build. His closely cropped hair gave him the look of a marine. He inhaled as all the color drained from his face.

Sebastian spoke to him with a tone of authority. "Say nothing."

Shade replied. "I don't think I shall have to. In her state, she could not handle the information. I think she is in shock." He turned and addressed me in a softer tone. "I am Shade. I am to show you to a guestroom. The vortex can be hard on someone who has never traveled in such a way. And before you say you want to go home, I should tell you that the only way back is through the vortex. We will explain in the morning." He offered me his hand and I took it.

As soon as our skin touched I knew there was something different about him. A strange hum made my skin tingle. I stared at his neck. No gills. I looked back at Sebastian. His were now gone.

Okay. I was losing my mind.

"No one here will harm you. I swear it."

"You say this after Ariel there tried to kill me."

"I am sorry about that. I will escort you to a place to rest. What are you called?"

A group formed around the three of us and I was out of options. "Gabriela. My name's Gabriela."

Sebastian barked at Shade. "Take her to the door."

Shade straightened and looked at me in a manner I could only call determined. What did these strange military men want with me?

I followed Shade into a large wall of rock. A crack wide enough for an army to march through acted as a passage into a small town. It was the most amazing thing I had ever seen—homes chiseled from stone with such detail it had to have been crafted by master artists.

Everywhere my eyes landed was something new and breathtaking. The most interesting thing was the floor. Although it was soft under my bare feet it appeared to be made of stone.

A thin vein of water snaked its way in front of us as if beckoning that we follow. I looked around for the source of the water but found none. The slithering trail led us to the most elaborate of the stone buildings. Scenes from battles were engraved on every visible surface. This place was no doubt important to the village.

We stopped and Shade motioned to the still-growing group of onlookers. "Gabriela? I…well…*We* would like to welcome you home."

Cheers broke out and I was ushered inside. Home?

GABRIELA

The door to my room was amazing. The frame was clear with large square gems of all colors that seemed to glow from within. It reminded me of the painted buntings. If the door was that beautiful, what would the room look like? I looked for a knob.

I turned to one of my escorts. "There's no handle."

Someone in the crowd yelled. "Stand in the light of the door." I could feel the anxiety coming off my audience in waves.

"Okay." I muttered. The light from the gems shone in a brightly colored pattern on the floor. When I placed my foot on the pattern, the door opened wide, and the mass of spectators gasped. A tall hooded figure in a dark lavender robe moved toward me with long sure strides. When it held up a hand, everyone went quiet. Instinctively, I knew whatever was under this getup was pretty badass. Slowly and discreetly, I tried to back my way into the room.

"Halt, young one," the robed figure said. The voice was female and firm.

I stopped moving at once. The crowd parted and lowered their eyes. I did likewise, hoping not to offend the specter in front of me.

"Lift your eyes to me, child."

Complying I watched as the form removed her hood. Feeling the color drain from my body, I was completely shocked at the touch of hands that steadied me. And her face.

"Your face," I whispered, shocked.

She smiled. Her skin was ebony and she was completely bald. Her eyes were the palest of lavender, almost white, and her lips the same lavender as her robe. She was the most beautiful being I'd ever seen. She appeared no more than me in age but her speech belied years maybe decades older. On the surface, we looked nothing alike but her bone structure was the exact copy of mine.

Tears glistened in her eyes and I raised my hand to wipe them away. "You are so beautiful."

"As are you."

"Who *are* you?" I asked. *What* are you? I wondered to myself.

Her lavender gaze, though kind, bore into me. "I am your aunt, Osun." When she saw my confusion, her face softened. "We will talk after your rest. Settle in your room and I shall explain in the morning."

I entered the room I was led to in a daze. I barely took note of the chamber. A massive canopy bed was set on a platform. Each of the four posts was the size of a large tree, but the carvings gripped my attention. Rose upon rose covered every inch of the posts, but that was where femininity ended. White walls and hundreds of candles gave the room a sterile feel.

Tomorrow was going to be a strange day.

GABRIELA

Warmth. I was wrapped in it. Burrowing deeper into the blankets, I tried to remember the last time I had such a great night's rest. The previous day's memories flooded my mind and I jerked myself upright only to bang my head on something hard.

I rubbed my skull and searched for the granite boulder I'd tried to chisel with it. Nothing was there. Then I saw it— a shadow on the bed sheet. I craned my neck to see a blue marble-skinned, black-eyed creature hanging upside down. I screamed.

Immediately, there was a banging at the door. I ran to it and stepped into the light. Four bodies fell into the room, one of them Shade. I pointed to the creature, and the group started laughing. I was very near panic. "Aren't you going to get it?"

While I stared in disbelief, Shade walked over to the bed and extended his arm to the creature. "Of course. Annihil, get down from there. Osun has been searching for you all morning."

Doing a flip any gymnast would be jealous of, this living gargoyle landed on the balls of its feet. If it were possible, I would have thought the beast was pouting. Looking at it right-side up, I could see it was not as big as I had believed. In fact, it was kind of beautiful in the way of a cobra. It stunned me by looking straight into my eyes. Suddenly, I was lost. I did not know what this creature was, but I loved it. It had taken just a look.

"Do you talk?" I asked.

"Yes, he does," answered Shade.

I gestured toward the creature. "With all due respect, I was not talking to you, Shade. What is your name?"

"An-Annihil." it replied. The voice was the voice of a child. Once again I was stunned.

"Annihil, I believe we have gotten off to a rotten start. I didn't expect anyone to be here when I woke." I knelt. "Please forgive me."

"It is okay, Sister. I scared you. Nunet said I was not to do that."

"Sister?" Somehow the title felt right.

Shade nodded toward the door. "We have already done enough damage, Annihil. Let's go before we are found out."

"Too late, Shade." The deity who claimed to be my aunt appeared. "You are dismissed. But I do ask a favor before you take your leave. Relay that my niece needs food and clothing."

"Yes, Osun," the guard said leaving with a bow.

"Wait a minute. Let's just hold on," I said, overwhelmed.

Osun turned to me. "Dear child, I would not hurt anyone least of all my own niece."

I blinked.

"No, I cannot read minds but I can read emotions amazingly well. We will tour the instruction domiciles and talk."

***

After I'd donned the clothes brought to me and I'd eaten my fill, Osun sent for me and we strolled through the strange place I had found myself in.

I glanced around at the edifices surrounding us. "What is this place? A military base?"

"We are Allu, my niece. Children of the moon."

I shook my head. "We're werewolves?!"

She chuckled. "No child. You definitely have my sister's sense of humor."

"Then what *is* an Allu? What makes you think I'm your niece?"

Osun did not respond. She guided me down another hallway carved from rock, on which hundreds of framed paintings hung. One stood out, larger than all the rest, and we stopped in front of it.

Three people stared out at me—two women on either side of a handsome older gentleman. The females were no doubt sisters. Their bone structures were the same and their eyes twinkled with undisguised mischief. The smirks on their faces were identical to the man's.

I looked at Osun in amazement. One of the girls was Osun. I did not need to be told about the other. It was like looking into a mirror. The only differences were her darker skin and amber eyes. I raised a hand to my own eyes.

"I take that back. I do not think I'm ready for this."

Osun nodded. "I understand, but it is time you learn the truth. No more hiding. No more being something you are not. You are Allu." She looked away and continued speaking. "Your mother wished for me to find you and I have done so. We will teach you more of who you are, but first, we must remove the seal she placed on you. It has been weakened by your presence here, but we need it completely removed."

"The seal?"

"Yes. Your powers are locked down."

"I don't have any powers."

"Of course, you do. You are Allu."

"You keep saying that!"

"The Allu are a race of beings able to control the earth's most powerful element. Water." She pointed to a smaller painting down the hall. "Your mother Nunet was the strongest of our kind. No one could match her skill in hand to hand combat or strength of will. She is a legend and hero among the Allu. She was a true leader."

"And my father?"

"Your mother kept him a secret." She paused, lost in thought. "I remember the day her aura changed. Everyone was frightened he would weaken her and put the entire tribe at risk. Yes, they mated, but she did not become his moiety. They never completed the bonding ritual, but I know she loved him very much. It was near the end of the war. It must have been hard for her. She became pregnant with you soon after meeting your father. The war had come to a stalemate, and soon after, Nunet disappeared. After a while, I received a note from her begging me to find you. She pleaded with me to love you as I would my own child. She failed to mention the seal of suppression."

She paused. "For years, we searched for you. There was no way to find you on land, so we had a conjurer try to invade your dreams. It was not until two weeks ago we received the sign of the prophecy. Your sign. It was then that we knew you were alive."

My heart was pounding. "My mother is dead? My dreams? I don't understand." I fell to the floor. This was too much.

She reached out to rub my shoulders, warming me. "Perhaps it would be better coming from a person you know." Digging in the pocket of her robe, Osun handed me a phone. "I understand this must be hard. But you had to learn who and what you are at some point. Call your human mother."

"Why?"

"She can tell you what you want to know. A seal of suppression is powerful. Its purpose is to conceal abilities. As a child, you would have exhibited some oddities. There is no doubt someone witnessed this.

"Moreover, although you might not have understood, you have probably seen the seal at work yourself. It is not meant to be used for long. Its purpose is normally to bind Allu children who have shown they are irresponsible with their bijous.

"Your mother modified the seal to hide your actual outward appearance. This modification was meant to be temporary. No one can hide who they are forever."

I was nauseous. In less than ten minutes, Osun had explained everything—my entire existence. I stared at the phone and then finally dialed my mom, all the while hoping she wouldn't think I was crazy and call one of those trucks with the padded walls.

"Hi, Mom."

"Hi, Droplet." Mom paused. "Whose number is this? Is everything okay?"

"Yeah. I was just wondering…" I glanced to Osun. "Mom, I was wondering… When I was a kid, was there anything else about me other than the crying thing? Anything strange, I mean."

Silence. I checked the phone's display to make sure she was still there. "Mom? Please. I need to know."

"Come home. We should talk about this face to face."

"What is it? What aren't you telling me?"

"I don't want you to think we were hiding anything."

I was beginning to get nervous. "What? I need you to tell me what you know. Please."

She paused again and then whispered, "You could do this thing with liquids."

"What? What could I do?"

"Make them dance."

"I'm sorry. Can you repeat that?"

"You could make liquid dance. Not a lot just… droplets." I stilled. "You could draw condensation off a glass to dance around the room. You could change the rain taps on the window panes to make music. You were blissfully happy when it rained because you had more droplets to play with.

"Your father and I didn't know what to make of it. He made me promise not to say anything to anyone. Then you stopped, and we just thought whatever it was had worn off. You never did it again and we left it at that."

"It never crossed your mind to tell me until now? Jesus! Here I am thinking I'm the only sane person in a town full of looneys." I made a face. "No offense, Osun."

"None taken," she whispered.

"Who are you talking to? Where are you?"

"Just my long lost aunt who's been searching for me for twenty-three years!"

I took a deep breath. "Mom, I love you but I'm going to need some time to process this. Swear you won't tell anyone about this conversation."

"I swear it."

"Good. I am going to learn everything about where I come from. And when I am done I will come home. We'll have a long chat. Got it?"

"Okay, but where are you?"

"I am safe. That is all I can tell you for now."

Osun left me to my own devices. In an hour, I'd learned more about myself than I had thought possible. I needed time to process it all. Osun's words rang in my memory. "No more being something you are not." Although it was weird, being here felt pure somehow.

Exercise had always been a getaway for me, so when I saw Shade walking down a corridor, I waved him down. "Please tell me where I can find a gym. I could really use a workout."

"If you ever need to find anything, all you have to do is call up the sechen."

"What is that?"

"Do you remember when you arrived there was a path of-"

"The water snake?" I exclaimed.

"Yes," he chuckled.

"Oh yes. Show me!"

"Well it may be hard for you with the seal still unbroken, but we can just—"

A path appeared. I wiped my palms on my thigh. "Did you do that?" I asked.

"No," said Shade. "*You* did. It took me months to master that."

I grinned. "Now what? How do I make it go?" At the moment it was weaving in and out of our feet.

"What do your instincts tell you?"

"I don't know."

"Close your eyes." My face warmed. My left foot stepped forward. "Open them."

I jumped up and down. "It's moving!!" I whooped.

Shade grinned. "You will know what equipment you require by how you feel around it. If you feel drained near something use it."

"Thanks, Shade. You have been a great help." I waved and followed the sechen.

The gym was filled with strange contraptions and there were no instructions. What on earth was I supposed to do? Everything I walked up to made me feel drained, just the opposite of what I had hoped. I closed my eyes as Shade had taught me and found no answers. Then I heard a familiar voice.

"Finally I can get my hands on you." Opening my eyes, I turned to see Sebastian leaning against a wall.

"I was completely wrong about you," he whispered. "I didn't think you were anything like Nunet but you could be her resurrected."

"The way you keep saying that is as if it's a bad thing."

"I don't know yet," he muttered. "We'll find out, though, because your training starts now."

"Training? For what?"

"The war."

"I am not fighting in any war. Whatever you people have going on has nothing to do with me."

"That is where you are wrong. Now that the seal Nunet cast on you is almost broken, you are as much a part of this as we are."

"Broken? Can that happen? Will I be able to use my powers then?"

"I'm not sure."

"How do I break it?"

"One of two things. The conjurer that created the seal for Nunet must be found or you must find your moiety. And it looks as if you have."

"My what? Moiety?" Thoughts raced through my mind. Cyrus had called me that word. How would Cyrus know what a moiety is?

I turned to Sebastian. "What does it mean?"

"Moiety means half a unit, a mate. Your moiety would be your husband, but it is more permanent even than that."

"Go on."

"It's the result of a ceremony between two lovers. The female must fully submit to accept her mate. Mind, body, and soul. If her mate is found to be unsuitable for her, he will live life as a eunuch. If he is accepted, the mates become bonded, you become moieties, and your lives are intertwined. When your mate passes into the next life so shall you. The bonding can never be undone and is intensely painful. Or so I have heard."

"Why? How is it painful?"

"When it happens, powers merge. Mates can become weaker or stronger depending on the individuals. Weakness is a phenomenon. Males usually become the more powerful of the two in order to protect their mate."

"We better find the conjurer fast. Being a moiety doesn't sound appealing."

"Tell me about it, kid."

"Wait. You said whatever my mother put on me is almost broken. What do you mean?"

"You have been going through changes, correct? You are no longer a child in need of protecting so the seal is thinning. If the suppression seal was working correctly your aura would have remained as human. But it hasn't. It tells us you have met your mate."

"What?" I shrieked in horror. *Cyrus.*

"Damn, girl, any higher and my ears would surely start to bleed. Our auras change twice. The first when we meet our mates. Think engagement. The second when we are bonded, as in marriage."

"I am not engaged. I don't even know him."

"Him who?"

That shut me up. Suddenly, I knew that I had to hide Cyrus from these people.

Sebastian's eyes narrowed. "Much like your mother indeed."

"Whatever. About this aura thing. How does it work?"

"It doesn't do much, honestly. Think of it as a wedding band. Unmated men know whether to stay away based on how bright it is."

"Why can't I see yours?"

"Males only have them temporarily. Plus, I haven't met my mate. There aren't many Allu women and finding a moiety is rare. As a matter of fact, your mother was the last of our people to do so."

"I thought their bonding wasn't complete."

"No one knows for certain."

Sebastian rubbed his hands together. "Enough with the questions. I haven't talked this much in a decade. What's most important now is finding a way to train you around the seal.

"Physical exercises would be at the top of my list. You aren't strong enough to lift a grape. When you pounced on me the other day, it felt like a house fly was attacking me." His grin made him look devilishly handsome. By the gleam in his eye, I knew I was in some serious trouble.

"Let's start your training."

"I will work out with you but I am not training. This is not my war." I was beginning to sound like a skipping CD. Sebastian had to be the most pig-headed man in all of existence.

"Osun would beg to differ. Why do you think I was sent to get you? You are the future of this tribe. We have no doubt you will be powerful. Your bloodline tells us so."

"What can you tell me about my bloodline? No one knows who my father is. He could be the weakest in Ellu's histories for all you know."

"Allu," he corrected.

"You know what I meant. How can the future of a race rest on one person's shoulders? Especially when that person didn't know the race existed a week ago. Four days ago my biggest issue was moving forward from the death of my best friend and defeating my nightmares. Now I feel like a well-rested Optimus Prime."

"Who the hell is Optimus Prime?"

"God, how old are you?" I scoffed, not expecting an answer.

"In human years, I am 51, but we don't measure time in the same way as humans."

"That's not... What?"

Shade entered the room, also dressed in workout gear. "It's all thanks to his bijou. It slows down aging. Our average sixty-year-old used to be around four hundred.

"Is it like being a vampire? The older you are the stronger you become?" I asked.

Sebastian chuckled. "God, no."

Shade frowned at him. "Don't dump all this information on the girl at once. You could have delivered that news a bit more delicately. Look at her. She is frightened to death now."

"Well, she asked."

"How would you feel if someone told you that you were human one day and the next you were something else? You look about twenty in human years."

The red-headed fiend shrugged. "She has to learn this stuff sooner or later, and Osun says we have to prepare her quickly."

I cleared my throat and both looked at me. "First, would you stop talking about me like I am not here? Second, I want to know everything about what I am. Third…" I said, grimacing, "I will make a deal with you. If you answer my questions I will do your training."

His savage smile told me I had just made a deal with the devil.

The day passed quickly after our pact. The history of the Allu was extensive and harsh. They'd been warring with the Phytian tribe forever. Moments of rest would be followed by the deaths of hundreds. Most were no longer sure what the war was about.

The most common thread was the Phytian kings. They were brutal men, who raided and killed as a show of power. The legend was that the first king found a way to meld together the weapons of both tribes. These weapons were called bijou. The beautiful crafted adornments were anything but simple pieces of jewelry as I'd thought—

they were weapons pure and simple. Wearing one magnifies the power within you.

"Think of it like this, Kid, without bijous, we are fighting in a nuclear war with pop rocks. With a bijou we have warheads. We all have the ability to manipulate elements, even humans. It is just we are smart enough to use it."

"I am human and I…"

"You are not human!" Shade and Sebastian said in unison.

"Sorry. Hard habit to break," I amended. "They make it so you don't age? Will I get one?"

They shared a look.

"What?" I asked.

"Depending on the strength of a bijou, the lifespan can be extended. They are typically passed down but it doesn't mean you could use it. Ultimately, the bijou chooses who wears it."

"Are they made by jewelers? Where do they come from?"

"A bijou varies according to the person. From a rock like mine to a single earring."

Just then it hit me. The story. The bedtime story my dad would tell me.

Sebastian glanced at me with concern. "You're looking green around the gills, kid. You okay?"

"Nunet…did she have a bracelet? A cuff with a big blue stone?"

Shade stilled. "Yes. Have you seen it? Do you have it?"

"No. And I'll tell you why," I growled. My dad had been right. However, the bracelet wasn't a simple clue. It was the answer.

When I finished the story, I wasn't the only angry person. Both Shade and Sebastian had come to the same conclusion I had. Someone knew who I was and had left me an orphan with humans after stealing my birth mother's bijou.

Later that night, I borrowed Shade's cell on the pretense of phoning my mother. It had been days since I'd contacted Cyrus and I needed to speak to him.

Had he known what or who I was? He had called me his moiety a few times which I could only conclude meant he too was Allu. For a moment I simmered, but the anger left as fast as it had come. How could I be mad at Cyrus for not telling me about another race? There was no way I would have taken him seriously.

The phone rang twice before Cyrus answered. "Shade?"

Now I was really confused. "No. It's Gabriela. How do you know Shade?"

"What are you doing with him? I have been losing my mind."

"I know I just vanished but—

"This is your second time doing this to me."

"I know what a moiety is. Are we mates?"

"Let me come to you. This is a conversation we should have in person."

"No. I can't think straight when you are near. Just answer the question."

Silence.

"Say something."

"I…where are you? I thought you were dead." Cyrus paused. "Listen, Gabriela, I need to know something. It is imperative you answer me."

"Okay."

"Is there a woman named Osun there?"

"Yes. Oh, thank goodness. I thought I was crazy. I thought I was stuck on some sort of weird reality show. The laws of physics do not apply here. There are red-headed men with gills. And…"

"Sebastian is there with you?" he growled.

"Yeah, he is a dick. I have a demon brother and he is…"

"Wait. Come again. You have a what?"

"My mother… Well, it is a long story. I am sure you know it."

"Gabriela, stop. I am overloading over here. Are you trying to tell me your mother was Allu?"

"Well yeah. I am like you."

"No, Love. You are human."

"No-o-o…" I drawled as if talking to a child. "I am an Allu."

"That is not fucking possible. How?"

When the story was out, silence greeted me.

"Cyrus?"

"They know you are mated. Have you told anyone about me?"

"No. I—"

"You have to get out of there. Gabriela, listen to me closely and follow every word or so help me God, I'll come to you myself!" I could hear the panic in his voice.

"I thought you would be happy to know I am one of you."

"But you're not," he said finally. "I am Phytian."

***

It was 10 o'clock at night and I stood just outside Allu territory. The rolling in of storm clouds told of a massive torrent approaching.

Cyrus was very specific with his directions. He was adamant I should trust no one. I'd managed to escape the watchful gazes of everyone by slipping out of a bathroom window. Cyrus was sure if they knew he was my mate, I would be imprisoned. He explained mates could not go long periods of time without contact. He believed the Allu would use me as bait to capture him.

If my choices were between my family and the Allu, the tribe stood no chance. Truthfully, the deciding factor was his vehemence Osun and Sebastian would keep us apart. There was no denying the deep pain in my heart at the thought. Honestly, how could I have fallen for a guy I hadn't known very long? But according to the Allu, mates had no choice in the matter.

Being away from him had been almost as terrible as grieving for Madison. My soul cried out for him nightly. There was no rhyme or reason to it, just a slow burning ache and a fear of becoming the person I was before. Cyrus completed me in ways I didn't fully understand. I hungered for his smile and the heat in his eyes. From everything Sebastian explained about mates and moieties, I knew this feeling would only grow.

At dinner, Osun had stated she wanted me to focus on my training. Training for a fight that wasn't my own was insanity—I'd never thrown a punch in my life.

My thoughts turned to Nunet. At some point, I knew I would start to resent her. Why bring me into a world where hundreds would look to me as their guiding light? How could I show them the way if I too was lost?

Three days of being in the presence of people with such strange gifts really opened my eyes. Humans, Allu and Phytian. The only differences being extra chromosomes.

The war between the Allu and Phytian closely resembled those of the human world. Instead of bombs and bullets they had their own talents, their own weapons. How could one person change the unchangeable?

"Gabriela. Hurry." *Shade?* "Don't just stand there, girl. Move your ass. Cyrus is waiting just above this hill."

"What? I thought he—"

"He will explain later. I know this is all new to you, but this act alone means I'm guilty of treason. From now until my death, my loyalties lie with you and your mate. You must hurry before we are caught. Go!" He turned me in the correct direction and swatted my backside hard. Twigs and large branches whipped at my skin and clothes as I tore up the hill.

"Over here," Cyrus called. I stumbled into his arms. Pulse pounding, I instinctively tilted my face up for his kiss. Though brief, it held so much promise there was no doubt in my mind what I meant to him.

"Sister, Sister, is that you? Osun had me looking all over for you. Here you are out in the dark making kissy noises with...Who are you?"

Annihil glared at Cyrus and Cyrus glared at him.

"What is *that*?"

"Don't hurt him," I said putting up my hands to protect Annihil. "He's with me."

Annihil spoke again. "Osun said to bring you back. I'm not 'pose to leave."

Cyrus sighed impatiently before reaching out to Annihil's shoulder. He'd done it so naturally, I thought it was a friendly pat, but that wasn't his plan. I watched dumbfounded as the demon instantly fell to sleep. Cyrus slunk him over his shoulder like a sack of potatoes.

"I told you not to hurt him," I snapped.

"He's just asleep," said Cyrus, dropping his burden in the backseat of his truck.

"How the hell do you know?" I hissed. A soft snore came from Annihil's lips. "Okay, but I'm sure we could have talked him into coming."

"No time," he said lifting me into the vehicle.

"Where are we going?" I asked.

"I don't know. I feel as if I know this land, but I have never been here. I can't explain it," he shook his head. "I only know the direction. It doesn't feel far." He stopped and looked at me. "I sound nuts, don't I?"

"Not at all. I trusted you to get me away from the Allu. Following your lead in a world I don't understand is no chore. You may have just saved my life."

Silence reigned while we sped through the night. Two hours passed before my nervousness subsided. "So I am not like you, huh?"

"No."

"Well, of course, I am not. That would have been too easy."

"I am not Allu. I am heir to the Phytian throne. We're a regular Romeo and Juliet." He laughed but his laugh wasn't pleasant. "Maddie was right. I *am* Dracula. I just kidnapped you yet again. And in the middle of the night, no less."

"You did not. I was a willing participant." I smirked.

"Stockholm."

"Sebastian says we are enemies," I whispered.

"Fuck that! You are *not* my enemy. You are my moiety."

I said nothing. Everything I'd learned told me of a future where few if any choices were your own in this supernatural world. Not even the person you would marry.

A loud bang woke me. Shafts of muted sunlight penetrated the truck's cab.

"Damn."

"What was that?"

"Tire blew. These are custom tires. I don't have a spare."

"I can call Triple A."

"Unless you can get them to swim across the Atlantic, we are walking."

"Wait. Where are we?"

"Morocco."

We pulled off onto the edge of the road. "Shade said there was only one way to get back home. He wasn't kidding. Speaking of him, how does he fit in to all this? How did he know what was happening last night?"

"Do you remember the name of the restaurant we visited on our first date?"

"No. Don't change the subject."

"I'm not changing the subject. The restaurant was called Shade's."

"You knew him? Did you know what he was? I mean did you know he was Allu?

"Of course."

"How are you friends? Why didn't you two kill each other?"

"War is what my father lives for. I, on the other hand, can do without it. I don't know why Shade hasn't tried to kill me. We will have to ask him one day."

Clouds quickly hid the sun as the storm loomed.

"We have to get going. We are almost there."

"Where?" said a groggy voice. "Hey… You didn't have to manhandle me. If Dedi goes somewhere I have to too. Nunet said so."

"Dedi?"

"It means infant or baby," Cyrus explained. "What else did she say, Annihil?"

"That my duty is to Dedi and her moiety."

I frowned. Cyrus just nodded.

"And she is my sister."

"How?" I asked.

"I don't know. Nunet just say it." I nodded and this time Cyrus frowned. As strange as it seems, he felt like a brother, like Trent.

There was no way to fix the tire. So we set out through the rain. Cyrus assured us our destination was close, though he still had no clue where we were going.

His skills were unbelievable. It was clear that, like Shade, he was a soldier. Never had he shared this part of himself, but it made me feel safe.

We entered a tunnel set deep at the base of a small mountain. It was astonishing to see Cyrus set a branch ablaze using only his mind. Deep inside the passageway a soft scratching echoed. The sound grew in volume as we traveled deeper.

"What was that?" I asked Cyrus.

"I don't know."

We continued forward and the scraping persisted. All at once the branch extinguished.

"Stay back," Cyrus demanded, pushing Annihil and I against the cave's wall. An eerie violet glow infused the tunnel's interior and fear caused my heart to accelerate. The illumination grew from tiny round pinpoints. Eyes. Hundreds of them.

More scratching reverberated off the walls and I held Annihil's hand tighter. Cyrus crouched into a defensive stance, his movement reminding me of a mountain lion.

As the source of the lights was revealed, bright violet rays expanded. Large scaly beasts, reminiscent of komodo dragons, covered almost every inch of the ceiling and floor. Strength poured off their massive bodies as they hissed a warning at us and my palms began to sweat. There was no way out.

The largest of the horde crawled down the walk. Its sharp talons scraped the rock in a hair-raising display of caution. None of us moved. Its mouth opened, revealing a chalky white maw and black tipped tongue.

I was about to reach out to Cyrus when a putrid warmth wafted across my neck. My heart pounded in my throat. I refused to move, but I knew I had to remain calm.

"Cyrus?" I whispered.

He whispered back without turning his head. "I know. Stay still."

I breathed slowly through my nose. Glowing eyes lit every corner and crevice but only the largest of the animals moved. It was clear there was only one alpha and he had challenged Cyrus. The beast hissed again and stiffened. Spikes slowly protruded through its leathery skin as it circled my mate. With a loud hiss, the beast attacked—raking and clawing at Cyrus's belly.

The animal was quicker than I could have ever imagined. Cyrus's well-placed kick sent the creature spinning in midair. It landed on its back but was on its feet within seconds. Putting as much room as he could between him and the beast, Cyrus dropped to the floor with a roll.

The animal hissed and Cyrus growled in response. They both leaped into the air in perfect choreography, crashing to the floor. Rolling over, Cyrus grabbed the beast in a bear hug and stood. A grotesque-sounding crack rang out. There was a ghastly twist to its claw.

The discordant note of the beast's scream caused its audience to hiss. Cyrus gently laid the creature on the floor. Laying his hand over the animal's wound, he released a roar that caused the hairs on my arms to stand up on end. The beast's pack slowly began to converge and Annihil dropped my hand.

"Stay where you are," Cyrus growled. He looked at me for the first time since the fight begun. His eyes had changed to the black I remembered from when we'd made love.

I took a step forward.

"No."

"Your eyes."

"Not now," he whispered, never taking his eyes off his opponent. He stood and the horde formed a circle around us. I shook as, in unison, every creature's head bowed in a signal of submission.

What the hell had just happened?

"This has something to do with my compulsion to come here," Cyrus said. "They no longer view us as a threat."

"How do you know?"

"The creature sent pictures to my mind."

"It can do that?"

"Yes. I have been found worthy to be leader of the swarm."

"Cool! So we can keep them?" Annihil asked.

"Well…yeah, I guess."

I shook my head wildly. "No. If I am going to be your mate and his…" I pointed at Annihil, who was now trying to climb onto one of the animals. "…sister. This is not happening. No way! Annihil, you get off of that thing right now! We are leaving."

Cyrus squinted. "I don't think it works that way. Whatever happened feels sort of permanent. Plus, they *are* pretty cool. The reason we didn't see them when we came in is because they camouflage naturally."

I was beside myself. "This is not cool. This is crazy. Do you realize that until a few days ago, I didn't know any of this world existed? Why is it you think I can handle so much new crap? I have powers I have never used, a mate I barely know—who is supposed to be my enemy, and a *blue* brother. And you think we are getting pets?" My voice reached an octave which could have rivaled Ariana Grande. "And I swear, Annihil, if you don't get down from that thing I am going to scream!"

"You are already," he muttered under his breath. Gripping my hand with a pout, we walked forward giving our new "friends" a wide berth.

Finally reaching the other side of the passageway, we entered a small abandoned village. It was another hidden world, but where the Allu living quarters were rooms inside caves, this was different—like a large apartment complex formed from rich soil. The mud appeared moist, but how could that be?

Cyrus moved quickly forward. "I thought you said you've never been here. Where are you going?" I asked.

"I don't know," he answered distractedly. "Orbin says no one ever comes to this place."

"Orbin?"

"The reptile," Annihil answered.

"How do you know its name?" I asked.

Annihil giggled. "He told us, duh?"

I rolled my eyes. "Is there food? I'm starving. Can I eat one of those animals? Wonder if this place has a kitchen."

"Apparently, Orbin can speak to me at will," Cyrus muttered. I wasn't sure he liked it.

After searching the place for any other surprises, we all found rooms of interest—for Annihil, there was an empty kitchen and a stocked garden. For Cyrus, there was the largest library I've ever seen, and for me, a nice balcony to read on. Cyrus brought me tea and a novel. I still don't know how he found such a pristine copy of *Tender Rebel*.

Most of the books were old or in a language I'd never seen before.

About two hours into reading, the romantic characters of the novel were no longer themselves, but us. I shook my head to clear it, only to have a flood of memories bombard my thoughts.

They were simple at first. Like the painted bunting visit, dancing at Club Sclavus, and the intoxicating scent of Cyrus's skin. But after a while, they spiraled out of control. Becoming more explicit with every scene. Moments later I had to put down the book. I wasn't concentrating anyway. I drank the last of Cyrus's tea and headed inside.

On shaky legs, I left the patio. *Cyrus's hot mouth on my neck.* I fell to my knees. I managed to pull a pillow from a nearby chair. Fitting it between my legs I squeezed tight. Specific parts of my anatomy felt like they would burst into flames. *Cyrus's tongue.* I moaned.

I covered my ears. "Make it stop. Make it—" *Cyrus's hands squeezing my waist as he thrust himself to the hilt.*

"My beautiful witch, you know what to do," Cyrus whispered from the door. I glared at him. He chuckled.

"That drink I handed you earlier was something I learned of in this place. It's an intensely powerful aphrodisiac." He shrugged. "I am not above fighting dirty to get what I want. This is just to amplify your mate's hunger. I can smell your lust in the air. You want me and you will be mine." He walked closer.

Cyrus gripping my hair tight as he pounded deeper into me. I rocked a little harder on the pillow. He reached me in the next second and gripped my hair, just as in the memory. Forcing me to focus my passion-drunk eyes into his golden gaze, he slowly reached down and I held my breath in anticipation. He snatched my surrogate lover away and released me.

Walking to a chair in the farthest corner of the room he sat with eyes burning. The air thickened. *The coldness of a countertop as he devoured me.* My eyes rolled back in my head.

"You will not!" Startled by Cyrus's demanding tone, I opened my eyes. One of my hands was kneading a breast and the other was halfway down my shorts. I put them at my side. I had to take control of myself somehow.

Cyrus said he'd done this. Get mad. Don't keep thinking of what his hands and body do to yours. Think about what you are going to do to him. Violence, that's the key. Think about wrapping your hands around his...*sitting slowly on his shaft.*

"No Gabby."

Again my hand was where it did not have permission. Not because Cyrus didn't want me to but because I was not going to pleasure myself while he watched. He chuckled again.

"Do you remember our first kiss? I do. You tasted so sweet, like nectar. I wanted to take you right there. I almost did. It was well worth the wait, remember? Look at you burning so hot for me. I could come just sitting here. Should I show you more?"

Yes. Do it now. "No. Go away." His shirt was off before I could finish the sentence. *Shit!* His chest was a weakness of mine. My favorite thing was to follow his scars with my tongue. My mouth watered at the thought of doing just that. He grinned the world's evilest grin.

"Cyrus…" I begged.

"Say it."

My clothes were becoming too heavy. Sweat bloomed over my skin and I started to shake. Cyrus stood gaining my attention. He unzipped his jeans and pushed them down his hips. His boxer briefs did nothing to hide his massive erection. I wanted that in my mouth. His eyes turned predatory and hypnotic. *Cyrus pinning me down with his teeth.* I can't take this anymore!

"Say it, Witch."

"Please, Cyrus."

"Tell me what I want to hear. Say it."

"Please. Make love to me." I whispered.

Everything stopped. An uncertain look crossed his face. I stripped out of my own clothes and knelt on the floor. I bowed my head in complete submission. Unexpectedly, I felt more powerful than I ever had. I knew that only I could bring him gratification. Cyrus would be mine as completely as I would be his.

Juices ran down my thighs. I didn't know how much longer I could go without some relief. My body began to tremble harder. He growled. The sound did not come from in front of me like I had expected but behind me. Chills ran over my skin but I knew better than to lift my eyes. After tonight we would be bonded. Certainly, I could not take any more of this.

"We will talk later." He gritted out. "Now, I will claim what is mine. We will not be apart ever again. You were made for me and only me. I will kill anyone who dares to touch you." The power he usually carried appeared to double with every passing moment.

The tiny hairs on my neck rose. Cyrus's hands were like open flames on my flesh. He guided my upper body to the floor as he lined our lower bodies together. I wanted to see him so badly but my ear was to the stone tile. The contrast of the coldness made my skin more aware. Something thick rubbed against my core. There was a moment of silence. I felt a flex of his fingers and with one powerful thrust he was inside me. His engorged manhood ripped a scream from my lungs while throwing me into one of the most intense orgasms I'd ever experienced. I thrashed and bucked. We needed to stop the pleasure from building in velocity and destroying us both. His fingers tightened on my hips as he started to move.

The rhythm was so fast and so hard that I began to shed tears from the pure perfection of it. With those tears, I released my last tie to self-preservation and surrendered completely. My back arched and another orgasm rolled through me an instant before Cyrus's roars thundered through the air. Every sensation increased tenfold as the impression of being ripped apart crept into my consciousness and then slowly, gradually, I was pieced back together. I was me again, yet different, better.

"Gabriela…" he whispered in a gravelly voice, scooping me from the floor.

"Cyrus. Did you feel it too? Did you?" I felt his nod.

"Yeah, Love. I felt it."

"Was that the bonding?"

"I think so. I mean you ARE reading my mind."

My eyes opened at that. The bed was soft. I watched his mouth closely.

"Are you there?" I thought to him. He grinned ear to ear.

"Yes, my lovely enchantress."

"No one told me about this part of bonding."

"No one told me either," he shrugged. *" but I would rather have you in my head than Orbin."*

"Cyrus?"

"Hmm?"

"Bonding was amazing, but let's not do that again. I don't think I would survive."

219

He chuckled aloud. "Okay. Happy wife, happy life, right?"

I nodded before drifting asleep in his arms.

"Wake up, Gabby. We have to move," whispered Cyrus.

He threw a pair of jeans and a t-shirt at me. I didn't bother to ask what was going on as I saw Orbin pacing with a limp. I winced. Whatever it was, it was bad.

Annihil rushed into the room a moment later. "Cain has tracked us to the forest outside the mountain."

I was confused. "Cain?"

"My father's tracker. The swarm saw him. He can only be here for one reason. I have to hide you."

"Why?"

"You are Allu. He would kill you on sight. Your seal has been removed."

"What?" Then I remembered Sebastian's words.

"I will explain later. Right now we need to get to the cellar. Annihil, you protect her. Remember what I showed you last night?"

"Yes." A look passed between them.

"Wait. *You* will come with us. Annihil is just a child— albeit not a *normal* kid but I will not let anyone harm him. Now start talking. What's going on?"

What Cyrus said next froze my heart mid-beat. "I think you are the next queen of the Allu." He pushed me into the library.

I turned to face him. "Are you serious?"

Cyrus looked up, ignoring me as he spoke to Annihil. Following his gaze, I saw there was a mural of a young woman. "Hurry, Annihil, climb up to the ceiling and push the fourth tile to the right of the eye."

Annihil obeyed, scurrying up the walls of the library. He slapped the tile Cyrus indicated and a large stone began to move in the center of the floor, revealing a spiral staircase. Annihil expertly dropped from the ceiling and landed, like a cat, on his feet. I shook my head. No matter how many times I saw it I would never get used to the fact he was a demon.

I went first, followed by Cyrus. After Annihil stepped onto the second step, the stone moved back into place with a soft click. As we descended, I saw what appeared to be light from somewhere in the tunnel. A mirror was angled to reflect the sun's rays. We followed the light which led us to a riverbank. The creatures waited for us.

I looked at Cyrus and frowned. In my mind, I spoke to him. *"Why didn't they attack Cain?"*

"I asked them not to. I can't have them in danger. Plus, if you are who I think you are, we are going to need all the support we can get. Stay low. Orbin is demanding they camouflage us from Cain and his men."

"Why is he looking for you?"

"I'm not sure."

"But you have an idea."

"I do."

Silence stretched as we crawled on our hands and knees between the creatures and into a dense forest.

Out loud, I asked, "How do we know Cain is not up here?"

"The swarm left a few behind to watch and relay details."

We followed the animals to a cave. It was dark but dry. Orbin's gaze cast a purple light in the cavern.

We sat on the floor to rest. Orbin made a noise.

"I don't know, friend," muttered Cyrus

"Huh?"

He gestured in the creature's direction. "Orbin wants to know where we should go. He says that we can't stay here."

"I know where we can go," said Annihil eagerly. "Osun!"

I shook my head at him. "No Annihil. No Osun."

"Why not?"

"Because Cyrus will be murdered on sight."

"Do not be silly," said Annihil. You are bonded. They kill him—they kill you."

I blinked. He was right. Osun would not allow anything to happen to me.

"I think he might be on to something," Cyrus said before I could. "We should try it. I will return you with the protection of Orbin and the others. Go back to the island. I will meet you there. I'm going to act lost and when Cain finds me I'll fly back home.

"I will contact you through Shade if I don't hear from you. Get them to open the vortex."

I cringed. Although swimming in the ocean no longer scared me, the vortex was a different matter.

"Can you do it?" He asked.

I nodded.

"That is my brave girl. We have to move."

With the assistance of the swarm, we made it away from Cain and said our goodbyes.

CYRUS

"Where the hell is she?" I hissed to no one in particular. I was prowling around the halls of the royal residence.

Teagan whispered when we reached the door of my chamber. "We will find her, Sire,"

When I returned Gabby and Annihil to the edge of Allu territory, there had been no sign of the tribe. Even Shade hadn't returned my calls. I received a strong feeling Gabby needed me, but after a few hours, the urgency eased.

I called Teagan and Niko to assist me in the search for the Allu and told them what happened. Yes, telling them was a risk but worth it in the end. Their loyalty was unswerving.

Niko entered the room. "Your father is requesting an audience."

"My father doesn't request anything," I grumbled.

Something wasn't right. I knew it as soon as I walked into his chamber. My mother sat to his right. I knelt. "Mother."

"Hello, Cyrus," sneered an all too familiar female voice.

I glanced to my mother's right and frowned. "Bianca."

"It is time for you two to marry," boomed my father.

I jerked my body upward. "The hell you say!"

Murdox glared at me. "You will be married tonight. It is the reason Cain went looking for you."

"What happened to your giving me free reign where Bianca is concerned?"

"I changed my mind once she explained about the human whore. I had Cain take care of it for you. It was a distraction."

"You had Cain take care of what?" I growled. I heard others echoing. I turned just in time to see Niko and Teagan step forward.

"Wow. That must have been some piece of pussy," said Murdox, observing my co-ruler and guard. "It matters not. Bianca, you may leave now. Your groom will meet you shortly."

Apparently, my face frightened her more than the orders my father had given. She appeared incapable of movement.

"Leave," I whispered, feeling Teagan gathering energy. He would kill her this time and accept my father's wrath if I didn't get her out of here now.

"Leave!" I commanded again. The urgency in my voice broke whatever spell she was under. Teagan moved to go after her and I gripped his arm hard enough to convey my emotions. "Later," my eyes read.

Bianca would die. I would make sure of it. My mother shifted in her chair and all eyes swung to her. Amaryl was never one to draw attention to herself.

Her beautiful eyes widened when they met mine, and her smile was so out of place, I flinched. She rose and walked to me and tugged on my shirt. I kissed her cheek.

"I love you, Dedi. Forgive me, but this is the only way."
Her eyes were filled with emotion. Without another
word, she followed Bianca through the door.

No one spoke for a full minute. I took a few deep breaths.
What the hell was going on?

Murdox finally spoke. "Your mother agrees of my
choice. Don't disappoint her. I will see you within the
hour."

I turned without a word. In my chambers stood a tailor
holding a tuxedo in his hand.

"You aren't really going to do this, are you?" asked Niko.

Teagan stomped around the room. "You should have let
me kill that cunt years ago! She won't get away from me
this time."

I took a deep breath. "I am going to renounce the throne."

Teagan was seething. "And as soon as you do, that bitch
is going to fucking die!"

"Get dressed you two," I said as calmly as I could.

"No fucking way," they snarled in unison.

"Please, grant me this last request as your prince."

Thirty minutes later, we stood in front of five hundred of our closest court members. Two of the three levels were filled with the purest Phytians. On the highest level sat the most royal including my mother and father. Tears shimmered in Amaryl's eyes. It was in that moment that I knew I could not renounce my crown.

The doors opened and Bianca entered. I glanced over and had to admit she made a beautiful bride, but quickly knew that she couldn't hold a candle to my witch.

While my head was turned a gunshot rang out. I snapped my head around. My father's arm gushed crimson. My mother held the smoking weapon in her hand. She pointed the gun at Cain, he froze. Amaryl giggled as she aimed it directly at his heart and squeezed the trigger. Without losing a beat, she swung the weapon back toward my father.

The look on Murdox's face was pure horror as my mother backed slowly to the railing of the balcony. Never lowering the gun, she reached into the bodice of her dress and pulled out a vial. She ripped off the top with her teeth and swallowed its contents. Hoisting herself over the railing, she turned the weapon to her own chest and fired. I stood in terror as my mother's limp form fell in a heap before me.

Chaos erupted. Snapshots of the day's events played like a slow motion film sequence. My father shot. Snap! Cain's face. Snap! The vial. Snap!

Suicide was uncommon to either tribe but rarer still to moieties, as when one mate dies, so too the other. Only in war had a moiety been known to do such a thing. I tried to think back. My mother seemed very different the moment my father announced my marriage to Bianca.

Forgive me but it's the only way, she'd said. Was this what she was speaking of? Suddenly, Bianca was by my side. "Darling, I understand that you have just lost your mother and father, but we really should marry. The court is going to be in an uproar?"

Niko stepped to my side. "Question, Bianca. When you ran to Murdox to tell him about Gabriela, did you stay and watch as her friend was mistakenly barbecued?"

"No!" she protested. A gathering of energy from my left told me I would not have to deal with Bianca again.

Niko continued. "Honestly tell me how you saw this working out for you. You thought you would take away Cyrus's mate before she could become his moiety?"

His words enraged me and I turned. The smell of ozone filled the chamber, and Bianca began to visibly tremble. "I...I...have no idea about what you speak of, guard. I knew someone died because of the fire but I didn't know it was her friend. I told Cain she did not live there." Her voice now shaking, she summoned her arrogance from where I know not. "Besides, why are you guys so upset? The human is not dead."

A rumble vibrated through the room.

"How do you know this?" hissed Teagan.

"Because when Cain broke into her house, there was evidence of where she might have gone. And he would have gotten her if the police had waited another day to do their job. I saw Cyrus carry her inside. I know the bitch lives."

The soft rumble intensified into a grinding purr.

It took me a moment to realize the animalistic sound I heard was coming from my own throat. A hard coppery taste filled my mouth and I stepped toward her. Heat infused my heart and sat thick in my throat.

I heard Tegan's voice as if in a distance. "Cyrus…"

My voice was rough when I spoke. "I warned you. You tried to have my moiety killed."

Bianca screamed. "She can't be your moiety. She is human!"

"That matters not," hissed Teagan, hurling an enormous ball of energy. I stepped into its path, absorbing the blow.

"She is mine." I roared. The chapel was emptied of all occupants. My mother's broken body still lay dead at my feet.

She dared to speak again. "Cyrus. I know losing your parents is hard."

I opened my entire being and the roar from my throat shook the walls with its ferocity. Red, white and blue flames ripped from my chest, incinerating Bianca where she stood.

For Madison. For Mitchell. For my mother. For my missing Gabriela. That bitch had breathed her last.

Once I regained control, exhaustion set in. My legs went limp and I crashed to the floor.

Teagan knelt beside me. "Wow, that's one way to get rid of her. I've never seen anyone literally breathe fire, especially without a bijou."

"Huh?"

"When you stepped in and absorbed my flame, your bijou flew off. It's on the floor by Niko's feet. And you wouldn't care to explain how you sucked up that fire, would you?"

I was fighting to stay awake. "I don't know," I whispered
In the end, I could only manage to say one thing.

"Home."

WINTER 1990

*A full month passed since his harpy left the note saying
she would return. In the beginning, Sorin thought she
might have changed her mind. Although the bonding
could not be undone, a different kind of separation was
possible. He felt as if his soul was being ripped to shreds.*

*For the last two weeks, he'd gone to town in disguise.
He'd thrown her name around in hopes someone would
know something about her but came up empty. After a
while, he could not risk being seen. It would put Amaryl's
life in danger and the safety of his mate was paramount.*

*Estivation was the only thing left to him. If she was being
harmed it would kill him, but perhaps he could find clues
to her location. He would hold on to hope. Morphing into
his true form, he rested on the dirt floor and shut his eyes.*

Four hours into meditating the mental torture began. The amount of depravity worldwide was appalling. Weeks felt like seconds as Sorin scoured every new wrongdoing. He discovered that he could choose not to focus on some of the scenes, and wasted no time thinking of the crimes against men. After another week passed, he found he was able to focus on a specific continent. The pain he felt was still great, but his emotions were not so bombarded.

By the sixth month, Sorin's worst fears were realized and he roared in fury. Amaryl was completely naked. She was chained to a wooden floor with links around her neck, shoulders, and wrists. A black box sat under her hips and her feet, also restricted by chains, were planted far apart. Her abused body and swollen abdomen were prominently displayed. Welts, grips, and other bruises covered her skin, but her mouth was the worst. A large hand print marred her jaw and lips, which were cracked and bleeding.

Sorin was outraged. To treat any woman in such a manner was horrific. But to do so to his pregnant mate made him homicidal.

"Sorin?"

He froze. He had to be hearing things. There was no way she could mentally communicate with him from this distance.

Yet her weak voice pierced the silence. "I love you. Never forget that. I'm sorry I made you claim me. I'm so sorry. Please forgive me."

"Never say that. Do you hear me? Never say that! I love you. I am coming for you. Can you tell me where you are?"

"No. Don't. They will kill you and if they do, we will die with you. Wait until our son is born."

He caught his breath. "Son?"

"Yes. He is like you. He speaks mind to mind with me." She paused. "Is that a Banumi trait?"

Sorin focused harder. "Yes. The Banumi were telepaths but only with their parents, mates and certain other species born within Banumi lands. No other species had this talent." It was all he could do to control himself. "I have to come to you. Where are you? Think, Love."

"I do not remember anything. I was drugged when they brought me here. Oh my God, Sorin. He… He raped me before my aura changed. Murdox thinks I'm his mate." The horror in her tone tore at his heart. "How long have I been here?"

"Banumi children are born at six months," he answered, but you have been there longer."

"Remember, our son is half-Phytian. We give birth around eleven months." She paused again. "Perhaps he will arrive soon. I've had a few contractions this week but my water has not broken. Murdox hasn't been back since his main purpose for me has been served. He thinks the child is his heir."

"If he has not been there, why are you in this state? Your body should have healed."

"Guards," she said.

***

237

After Cain kidnapped Amaryl, she'd awakened in this room. In the first two weeks, Murdox raped her repeatedly, sometimes sleeping on top of her.

She had tried to tell him that she was claimed, that he was making a mistake, but all that had earned her was a gag. Once her aura changed he convinced himself she had willingly submitted to his dominance, and when he realized she was pregnant he left her alone but had given his guards permission to humiliate her.

They had used her as their personal peep show, slipping into her cell and masturbating over her twisted body. Murdox had forbidden them from entering her. His fear was they might hurt his heir.

The worst of her visitors was Cain. He would not touch or expose himself. He did not beat her or talk. He would simply sit and stare at her body and then, before leaving, he would force her to climax.

She did not know how she'd managed to stay sane. When her son first connected to her, she thought her sanity had finally left her. Immediately, she knew he had his father's spirit. She knew Sorin would be proud to know his son. A familiar stirring in her mind gave her hope.

While communicating with Sorin, she realized her hope was misplaced. She needed to give birth before he came to her. If anything happened to the two of them, she needed her son to be safe. Even if Murdox managed to kill them, their son would be raised as the heir to the Phytian tribe.

Tuning her mind to the child, she called for him. Since he did not yet understand language, they communicated by impressions. She sent messages to him to move down into the birth canal, but because of her chains, he could not.

She moaned as loud as she could, gaining the guards' attention, and told the child to keep moving. He did as she asked and soon her water broke. The guards' faces drained of color and she screamed louder as a wave of contractions took over her body.

The cell door opened and an older woman dressed in a conjurer's traditional garb was pushed into the room. She gasped at the sight of Amaryl and rushed to her, yelling something to the guards.

Moments later, Murdox burst into the room, loudly cursing. Guards rushed in to unchain her and remove the box beneath her. The relief was so great, she drifted into unconsciousness.

***

Powerless, Sorin had watched all from his cave. He knew Amaryl plan. She wanted their child to live and would do everything in her power to have it so. She still thought she could hide things from him, but not so—they were of one mind. He knew he could never make it to her in time and he too needed to secure their son's future. The child would know the truth of his birth and parentage.

Sorin quickly broke out of his trance. Morphing into his human form, he summoned his sword. Festakio was like no other. It was made of special uranium from the most sacred of places. Generation upon generation passed down the royal weapon—it could only be wielded by those in the bloodline, and when called, it bonded itself to the arm of its master.

Slicing across his chest as deep as he could, Sorin whispered ancient words in his native tongue. An *inscription appeared on the blade in vivid gold. Kneeling to the dirt floor he sliced deep across the earth. He spoke more Banumi commands, and tar poured forth.*

Sorin covered the blade with the blood of the earth and then, taking a much shorter blade from his boot, he cut through muscle, arteries, and tendons to remove Festakio from his flesh. Opening a pit in the ground with his mind, Sorin stepped in and covered himself with dirt. He did not know if what he was asking of nature was possible but he had to try.

Chanting, he gave himself over and became a part of the earth itself. When his request was answered, the earth opened and air was forced into his lungs. He could not rest—he had to connect with his mate. This time, finding her was easy. Her eyes opened and she saw straight into his soul. Together they mentally coached their son into the world.

The healer was sympathetic to Amaryl. She wrapped the child in a towel and prepared to hand him to his mother. The child was jerked away and handed off to a guard.

Hatred burned so deep in Amaryl's eyes, Murdox took a cautious step back.

"You will terminate my mating, Conjuror," said Murdox.

The healer shook her head. "I cannot do that without killing one of you and damaging my soul in the process. Breaking the tie between you goes against the laws of nature. I would be latching my life to the one who passes. I could die."

"We will just have to take that chance, Natalia. And if you kill me, you will regret it. Get to work." Turning to Amaryl, he smiled. "Thank you for giving me an heir. Unfortunately, I do not think this relationship is going to work."

Amaryl mumbled something and Murdox frowned. Grabbing her jaw in his hand, he forced her mouth open and leaned closer. "Repeat that," he growled.

"My son is the sole owner of my bijou." With all of her energy, she spat on his cheek.

Murdox staggered back, wiping the spit from his face. "You bitch. You really are my mate. Fighting to the end.

If you weren't so used up I might have kept you. Your bijou holds little power compared to mine. It is a wonderful gift you have given my son."

He turned to Natalia. "Are you ready?"

She nodded.

Amaryl mentally reached for Sorin.

Sorin growled into Amaryl's mind, "The breaking of a claiming is not possible."

"It doesn't matter, my love," said Amaryl, as the conjuror plunged a knife into her heart.

The conjuror coughed and blood poured from her mouth.

She turned to Murdox. "You must be the one to pull the blade from her body."

In one motion, Murdox ripped the blade from Amaryl's chest and sliced open the healer's throat. When he saw the look on her face, a mad grin crossed his own. "Don't look so shocked, Natalia. I can't have this story circulating. People would think me cruel."

He spun around and looked at Cain. "Remove these bodies and bring in our other new guests."

The echo of his words was the last thing Sorin and Amaryl heard before death took them.

GABRIELA

Sebastian paced in front of me. "We have been looking everywhere for you. Where the hell have you been? And why did you have Shade tell Osun to meet you here?"

"Why are *you* here? I only wanted Osun." I watched as his eyes narrowed.

"You are bonded," he hissed. "Who *is* he?"

I ignored him. "Where is Osun?"

"I am here." Osun broke through the brush.

Our meeting place was on a hidden stretch of beach Annihil led me to. He tried to convince me I would not need an exit but I had wanted one in case things went south.

Osun searched my face and frowned. "Sebastian and I broke up to find you more quickly. Are you okay?" Her eyes swung to Sebastian with a question. He nodded. She turned back to me. "You have a moiety?"

"Yes."

"Is this why you hid from us?"

I nodded, and she spoke again. "We cannot harm him. He is your mate."

"He is Phytian." Silence.

Then Sebastian roared. "You have got to be fucking kidding me! After all the things you know, how could you turn on your own people?"

"He is not like that!"

Osun spoke. "Sebastian, we are strangers to her. We could not expect her to give up her life."

Her words stung me. I no longer considered them strangers. I understood they were my family, but the tie to Cyrus was more important. I needed to get the meeting over with and head to the estate. "Look I have to go. I just needed a place to be for an hour or two. I also wanted you to know I'm okay."

Sebastian stepped closer. "You aren't going anywhere. And you will tell us who you are bonded to."

"I will not."

He moved closer still. "Oh, you *will*."

Osun gasped. At that moment, the swarm chose to reveal themselves.

Sebastian didn't appear to notice. "The enemy has murdered everyone we have known and loved, including your mother, yet you have turned whore for one." He took another step. His arm shot out to grab my wrist in a punishing grip and a chorus of hisses erupted. Sebastian glanced around only then noticing our new guests. Teeth bared, he ordered, "Call them off."

Before I could speak, a louder and much closer hiss silenced the swarm. A cold sweat rolled down my spine. This time, Sebastian released my wrist and slowly backed away. When he made it to Osun's side, I gathered enough courage to look at what had frightened him.

Annihil stood strong, his once cobalt skin glowing a flaming orange, his eyes focused solely on Sebastian. His four front teeth had sharpened into daggers. Sebastian leaned to whisper in Osun's ear and Annihil hissed again.

But no matter—Osun's eyes were focused on me. Nothing Sebastian was saying was registering.

I locked eyes with hers and the moment I did, a wealth of information flooded into my mind. Osun's eyes widened. "This has never happened without prompting."

Knowledge bombarded my brain with such force, I doubled over to vomit. "I will try to slow or stop—"

Annihil growled and his tone brooked no argument. "You will do nothing."

Osun pleaded. "She could die! We must stop this!"

If it were possible, the barrage of data accelerated and Osun fell to her knees. A thin trail of blood leaked from her left ear.

Sebastian knelt to comfort her and my vision became hazy. I could barely make out shapes as the swarm formed a circle around me. With every second the download went faster until just as suddenly as it had begun, it ceased, slamming itself behind an impenetrable wall.

It took me a while to realize that the pain in my head was gone. I stood wiping my streaming eyes with the back of my hand and looked toward Sebastian, who was supporting a weakened Osun. When our eyes met, he flinched.

My gaze flicked to Osun for an explanation. I cleared the hoarseness in my voice. "I know I have something powerful now."

Osun lifted her head. "It has locked itself away in your mind?" When I nodded, she smiled, almost in triumph. "It is the histories. You mustn't tell anyone except your moiety."

Sebastian was incensed. "You are allowing her to betray us?"

Osun glanced at him, waving her hand toward Annihil and the swarm. "She cannot betray people she does not know. There is more at work than we are aware of. Look at her."

Sebastian growled but said nothing.

Osun looked back to me. "Gabriela, you must come back to us with your mate. I guarantee no harm will be done to you or yours. But there is still much more you must learn." She looked away. "We carry the same burden now. You are needed more than you could understand."

As never before, I knew I could trust her. "I will return," I promised.

Sebastian spoke. "I will go with her."

"No!" commanded Osun. "You must stay here. There are new matters we must attend to. She will be perfectly safe. Of this I have no doubt," she said, glancing down at Annihil. I looked too. He had returned to his calm cobalt. "I tend to forget you are the wise one," she said.

Annihil giggled and Osun turned back to Sebastian. "Open the vortex and take them to Gabriela's home. If you do not come back, I will come after you myself."

Grumbling, Sebastian put his bijou in his mouth and sprouted gills right in front of my eyes. Annihil and I followed Sebastian into the sea, and when the vortex opened, Annihil held my hand and tugged me into it.

In a flash, we were back at the dock near my house. Dizziness swamped me as I dragged myself onto the pier. To my surprise, Orbin and the swarm were with us. In the water, the creatures were visible, but back on land they

became camouflaged.

A curse to my left reminded me Sebastian was still near. I glanced over just in time to see him give me a look filled with hate.

I swallowed hard and mumbled, "I think I just made a new enemy."

"He'd better hope not."

The back door of my house was still unlocked but nothing had been tampered with. I sighed with relief. After fixing Annihil a feeding-trough-sized helping of double fudge, I showered, trying to wash away the events of the day. I couldn't shake the memory of the blood running from Osun's ear. After drying and applying toothpaste to my brush, I reached to wipe the condensation from my mirror, only to find it had vanished with the thought. I leaned forward, nose all but touching the mirror. What the…

"Annihil!" I screamed tossing on my robe and hurrying back to the kitchen, but he wasn't there.

He yelled from another room. "Your yelling is making me miss the best part!"

I followed Annihil's voice to find him and Orbin in the den. Popcorn and ice cream containers were strewn all over the floor. A rerun of RHWOA played loudly on the television.

"My eyes," I pointed.

"What about them?"

"Don't you dare act as if you don't know what I'm talking about. You tell me right now."

Annihil shrugged, still watching television. "It is not as if they changed completely. They won't do anything freaky like turn into slits or glow purple or black like your mate's. But they will have a purple ring around them." He spoke as if the change would have no real effect. For a being with blue skin, I guess not.

I grabbed the remote and turned off the television. "I want you two in the car in ten minutes. Cyrus must be freaking by now."

We made it to Cyrus's estate, just in time to see Teagan and someone else carrying him inside.

NIKO

We reached Cyrus's bedroom. "What the fuck are we going to say to her?" said Teagan.

"Nothing. We aren't going to say anything. Quick, help me strip him."

As we tossed shreds of fabric to the floor, Teagan hissed again, panicked. "That isn't going to work, Niko."

"It will if you keep your mouth closed. Our loyalty is to Cy, not her. Stop being such a coward. If he wants her to know, he will tell her when he wakes."

I had just switched off the lights when Gabriela reached the hallway. Teagan stepped into the doorway and she tried to push past him. "What happened to him?" she demanded.

I locked eyes with Teagan. Although it was clear Gabriela and Cyrus completed their commitment ritual there was something about her which made my internal alarms go haywire. Cyrus's mate was no weak woman.

Teagan said nothing.

Gabriela glared at both of us. "Did you not hear me? What happened to him?"

Teagan took a step back. "Listen, Gabriela, I'm not sure we are allowed to tell you. Honestly, we don't know."

"What do you mean you're not sure if you can tell me? I am his mate!"

"I understand your frustration, but we can't tell whose side you're on."

The moment the words were out of his mouth I knew he'd made a mistake. So did he. Gabriela's aura began to change—one minute it was normal and the next it swirled with black and lavender. Her body stiffened and somehow she managed to suck half the house's oxygen into her lungs.

I felt a tug on my shirt and looked down. There stood the ugliest child I'd ever seen. And it was blue! Baring the most deadly-looking teeth I'd ever seen, it said, "He shouldn't have said that. I would move out of her way if I were you."

"Kid, you are one creepy-looking S.O.B.," I said backing away.

"I know," it said, with a decidedly less canine smile. The creature walked to Gabby, kissed the back of her hand and tugged her through the bedroom door. Her ranting stopped almost instantly and her aura evened out, but her acidic glare made me feel as if a bucket of crap had been dumped onto my head.

The ugly kid was right. A mate's loyalty is not to be questioned.

CYRUS

A large blob of blue was the first thing I saw upon waking. I squinted.

Annihil squawked. "He's awake!"

I grimaced. "Shut your damned mouth or I will skin you and wear your bright blue hide as a button down."

Niko's voice pierced through the haziness in my brain. "I tried to tell it not to stand over you like that.

I blinked trying to clear my vision. "It's okay. He has no concept of personal space." I inhaled and blinked again. My vision choosing that precise instant to clear, I beheld my own personal angel. My moiety, my witch.

"You are so damn beautiful," I breathed. She smiled and it melted my heart.

I heard the clearing of a throat and looked past her to the person who stood directly behind.

It was Teagan. I nodded to him and whispered, "My brother."

He came at me with such force I didn't have enough time to brace myself. His hug was so strong, I felt vertebrae cracking all the way down my back.

"You are going to be okay," he said. "You hear me? You're going to be all right."

I pulled myself free of his grip. "Okay. Get yourself together, will you?"

My voice broke. Emotions were roiling within me. I focused on my senses to regain my composure. The scent of beef permeated the air, causing my stomach to howl. I watched in stunned amazement as Gabriela, Teagan and Niko all rushed to the door.

Gabriela rolled her eyes at the others.

"Where do you two think you're going?"

I gawked as my toughest and most brave warriors stopped cold and turned back to me. I looked at Gabby and raised my eyebrows. "You've broken them."

"Did not. They're still your obedient pets. Sit tight. I'll be right back with food."

When she cleared the room, I looked at Teagan and Niko. "Obedient pets?"

Teagan looked sheepish. "She is still mad at us for not telling her why you were in this condition. Seeing how we are confused about what happened too, we decided you should be the one to tell her."

Niko chimed in. "By the way, your mate can be right frightening when pissed."

My lips twitched and my amusement fled when I registered what he was saying. They hadn't told her what happened. I cursed and nodded, remembering times past. "Yes, she can."

Until then, Annihil had been quiet. "We have a few things to tell you too." Whatever it was Annihil didn't like it. For one brief second his skin flashed bright orange.

I cursed again.

All four of us were silent when Gabriela returned. I watched her throat move as she swallowed and lowered her head. She'd done the same thing when I'd called her beautiful before. I thought she was nervous because of our audience and touched her mind without warning.

She gasped and her eyes flew to mine. I saw everything that happened to her. Sure enough, Annihil's words were true. Rage filled me. I should have gone with her.

"You can't be angry with yourself," said her voice in my mind. Shaking my head, I lifted my hand to her face. "Let me get a better look," I said aloud.

The men moved to the other side of the room. Her eyes had always been lovely to me, but I had to admit the tiny ring of lavender brought out a new depth. "What caused the exchange?"

"I'm not sure," she whispered.

"Your eyes are beautiful," I told her, opening myself up. I wanted her to see I spoke the truth. She smiled. I asked a few more questions before it was my turn to share.

When I was done, I had come to know with certainty two things about Gabriela. One, she was head over heels in love with me. Two, she was frightening as hell when pissed.

I told her the events with my mother. I felt her every stab of shock, every prick of pity and flame of fury. Her tears flowed unchecked down her face. When I got to the part where Bianca was still trying to get me to marry her while my mother's body lay only a few feet away, the most amazing thing happened. Gabriela's tears hardened like glittering diamonds. They spun wildly around me in a display of power I'd never seen.

Teagan and Niko moved toward her but I shook my head. She was trying to protect me—I could feel it in her mind. At that moment, I felt no remorse at killing Bianca. She was the reason my moiety's friend was dead.

There was only one way to calm her. Continue the story. I left out nothing. As I talked, her spinning tears slowed then stopped, falling and melting where they landed, and I pulled her close to me. I needed to hold her. By her shaking, I could tell she needed the same.

The room was silent for a while when suddenly, a chorus of hisses rattled the windows.

Teagan jerked around. "What the hell is that?"

Annihil giggled. "Security." I laughed too. So much happened I neglected to tell Teagan and Niko about the swarm.

Orbin touched my mind, warning that he thought an intruder was present. I directed Niko to check the premises. Niko returned, stating he'd found nothing.

While Niko was gone, Teagan told me that Amaryl's body had remained untouched. Murdox's and Cain's had obviously not been so honored. Massive amounts of blood were found where they had been seated. Images of people saving skin, hair, and bones as souvenirs danced around in my mind. My mother was loved by her subjects. Murdox had not.

I gave Teagan orders to plan the pyre ceremony for my parents. "It needs to be held immediately. Order must be restored."

"Can I come?" Gabriela asked.

"No," I said solemnly. "The tribe is already in turmoil. Finding out that their new king is moiety to an Allu would start a civil war. As it stands, there are likely some who already think I am weak because of this loss."

I thought for a moment. "This is a dangerous time. My great-grandfather came to power by killing the previous king. Someone could be plotting my downfall as well."

It would take another day of eating and sleeping to get my strength back for the ceremony. Hundreds attended, all with forlorn faces. Their glances, filled with pity and sympathy, began to make me nauseous. None of these people actually gave a damn. They just wanted to be seen. Showing up in their finest dresses and tuxes like the death of my parents warranted a fucking cocktail party.

Inhaling deeply, I tried to shake off the negative thoughts. It was, after all, their right and duty to mourn their leaders. I approached the pyre and questions swirled in my head. Amaryl had never been a violent woman. Even if she had been, why had she chosen that particular time and place? Why such a method? She drank poison, shot herself and then plunged two stories. At my *wedding*.

The pyre tradition of the Phytians was to toss gold dust into the blaze to purify the soul on its journey. Each person who passed whispered a chant of farewell. Flecks of the precious metal danced in the firelight. The dark sky swallowed the smoke and ash like a sacrificial offering to the gods. Stars above appeared dimmer as if they too mourned.

Looking out on the sea of faces, I took a deep breath and knelt. Shocked murmurs hummed among the crowd. There was no greater honor than for a king to bow to his court. I stood and watched shadows from the funeral pyre morph and twist.

"Sire?"

I spun around, almost knocking down the tiny woman behind me. It was Niko's mother, Maria. "You spooked me," I said, steadying her.

"It is quite all right to be off your game on a night like tonight, Cy."

I smiled at the nickname. Maria and her son were the only people outside the family I allowed to use it so freely. My mother had employed her as a maid but they had grown to become best friends.

"Did you wish to speak with me?"

"Yes, Sire. I know this is an inopportune time, but I was given strict instructions by Amaryl." She handed me an envelope and my mother's bijou. My name was written boldly across the front of the envelope in Amaryl's hand.

Maria apologized again. "I didn't know what she was going to do. I was to give this to you after your wedding, but..."

Her sorrow was palpable. I leaned down and put my arms around her. "This was not your fault, Maria."

After a few more words of kindness she left. I stuffed the bijou and envelope into my pocket and was quickly surrounded by others wanting to give their condolences. After an hour of accepting handshakes, hugs, kisses and food, I was exhausted. Seeing it, Niko came to rescue me. We were back at home and I was soaking in my massive tub with my angel before I remembered the exchange and the conversation with Maria. My expression must have changed because Gabriela was quick to notice. I tried to block her from my thoughts.

"What is it?"

"Nothing." I didn't want to ruin the momentary taste of peace with reality.

"Don't tell me that. You just threw me out of your mind. Not to mention the fact that your body has stiffened into stone."

I planted kisses under her ear and followed a line to her collar bone. "I didn't realize. How can I make it better?"

She pushed me away. "You can tell me why. Stop trying to distract me."

I sighed and launched into the story. "My mother left me a note and her bijou. Niko's mother — her best friend — gave them to me at the ceremony."

Gabriela sat up. "What does the note say?"

"I didn't read it."

"Why the hell not?"

"I forgot about it until just now."

Gabriela stood up in the tub and waited. "Come on," she demanded.

My eyes traveled up her soap-slick skin. When I got to her face I knew my thoughts were written on my own. "After," she whispered.

I cursed and followed her. I reached for a towel only to notice I was completely dry. Raising an eyebrow to Gabriela, I wrapped the cloth around my waist.

"I have been practicing," she explained.

I chuckled at her guilty expression and stepped out of the tub. Amaryl's letter and bijou were still in my jacket pocket. We sat on the bed.

"Whatever is in there we will handle it together," she said. Nodding my understanding I started to read.

Dedi,

Someday you will forgive me. As the future of the tribe, you are the key to understanding the severity of our war.

This was the only choice left to me. Please do not mistake my words as the rantings of a mad woman. The lies I have lived with for so long were starting to eat away at me. I could not survive thinking you would live as Murdox and I have. My actions will put into perspective how vile and depraved Murdox truly is. This was the only way to stop his manipulations.

Although you are my blood, you are not of my flesh. Before I go further, let me say that you may not be my son by birth, but the love I feel for you would rival that of any natural mother. I love you more than words. More than all the stars in the sky. You are my heart, my very breath. Anything I am has only been with you in mind. I count myself fortunate, extremely blessed to watch you grow into the great man you have become.

The Phytian and Allu cannot continue as they are. Our existence will become a falsehood, a farce of what we could be. If you do not act now, not one, but both tribes will be destroyed.

Although I have gone, remember that there is always a purpose for the things we do.

Love,

Anabel Kier

I couldn't believe what I was reading. "What does she mean I'm not her son?! Anabel? Who is Anabel?" I whispered. My mind raced, trying to assemble what she was trying to tell me into something that made sense. I had inherited many of her features. From the thin nose bridge to the hair color and skin tone. How could there be any doubt? It was impossible to have children without your mate. I was clearly Phytian. I had a *bijou*. I held hers up and examined it—it was almost identical to my own.

I felt Gabriela piecing the puzzle together with me. I grabbed on to our mind link and let her examine everything I knew.

Her eyes narrowed. "Cyrus, how did you get your bijou?"

Following her thoughts, I went to my desk and withdrew mine from a secret drawer.

"Shade told me bijous are typically passed down. The weapon chooses who wears it. It is not always a special made thing. It can be something specifically for you, like a rock. Just because one is passed down to you doesn't mean you can use it."

"I know!" I snapped, but she continued as if I had not spoken.

"You've had yours since birth. Your mother still had hers and so did your father. How could that be?"

An idea formed in my head and I began to shake. Gabriela approached my thoughts cautiously. In our linked minds, I saw she understood what direction my thoughts had taken. Gently taking both bijous in her

hand, she did something I'd been far too afraid to do—
interlock them.

A bright light flashed from the gems and what had once
been two separate pieces merged into one. In its new
form, it was too small to place around my neck.

"Hold out your arm." She said.

She slid the weapon onto my wrist. A piercing agony
rushed up my veins on contact. From a distance, I heard
Gabriela scream. I tried to get to her but couldn't. After
some period, the pain subsided. I was drenched.

"Why am I so wet?"

I heard Niko's voice. "You were on fucking fire." He and
Teagan stood in the door supporting Gabriela, who had
passed out. I jumped from the bed and raced toward her.

"No." Niko snapped. I stopped.

"What did you just say?"

"We don't know what the fuck is going on, but whatever
it was nearly burned the house down. Gabs here is the
reason we are not all standing in a pile of ashes. She

drained herself completely in order to contain your flame. Get yourself under control asshole."

"I wasn't angry when this happened." I started to explain what happened with the bijous when Gabriela came to. I gently picked her up and laid her on the bed.

She opened her eyes and looked at me. "Are you all right?"

"Am *I* all right? You are the one who fainted."

"Let me see it."

I held out my wrist, but I could see nothing there.

Gabriela touched the underside of my arm. "Look."

I twisted my wrist and stared. Thin lines of gold snaked in a pattern under the skin of my forearm.

"Jesus!" Teagan yelled from behind me. "You know what? I am so done trying to figure out whatever this is. I am going back to my room to make love to my moiety."

"I am right there with you, bro," said Niko. Teagan blinked. "I mean I'm done with this craziness too. Not the part about Bella."

Gabby watched as my two friends cleared the door. "Why didn't you tell them?"

"For what purpose? Both Amaryl...I mean Anabel *and* Murdox are dead. Telling them now would just create questions I don't have answers to. Perhaps I never will. If this information about my parentage got out my people would be in danger. Battles would break out and many would die. It is unnecessary.

"It will take time, love, but as soon as a peace treaty is signed with the Allu, I want to marry you in your way, both as a human and an Allu. I want you by my side." I knelt and asked my angel to marry me. She nodded with tears in her eyes. I swallowed her yes with my kiss.

SOMEWHERE IN PHYTIAN TERRITORY

Blood dripped from my blade onto the toe of my boot. Maria's incessant wails grated on my nerves. She was securely chained to the stone walls of my hideaway, but it hadn't kept her quiet. Even so, I had to admit the old woman was tough. I'd worked her over for an hour cutting her all over with shallow slashes. Her moans made my cock hard. She wasn't attractive but she had two holes that were tight enough. Her body shivered from cold and fear.

I drove my knife deep into her thigh. She felt it immediately. I whispered under my breath. "Shut up, whore."

Her screams turned into whimpers. God she was ugly. Blood and sweat were the only things covering her body. Since the slut, Anabel, had played her trump card I'd been in hiding. If the people of my court knew I lived things could get a bit dicey. Maria here was the key. "I will ask you only one more time," I demanded. "What did you give to my son?"

She whimpered again. "Please, Sire. I speak the truth. It was only a sealed envelope and Amaryl's bijou." Her tears made my cock throb and I slowly undressed, revealing my body's condition. Her whimpering became louder and I looked down at the floor. She'd pissed herself the first time. I chuckled, wondering if I could make her do it again. I stared into her eyes until she lowered her head in submission. My growing gratification was quickly dash as she inhaled and released a soul tearing scream for help.

Panicked that someone would hear, I drew the blade across her throat and her screams went silent. I bellowed in rage as I entered her corpse.

Leaving her used body hanging from a wall, I picked up my bag and vanished into the night.